Fabulous Fathers

"Then why don't you marry me, Clay?"

Shock, like a bolt of electricity, immobilized him. "Why would you even consider being my wife, Tamara?"

Tamara's blush turned from pink to red, but she didn't try to look away. "Because I...I love you."

"But you've known me for such a short time. I suspect that you feel sorry for me because I'm a widower raising my child alone, and I know you're fond of Francie—"

"I adore Francie," she interrupted, "but that has nothing to do with my feelings for you."

"Forgive me if I sound like I'm bartering for a corporate merger instead of a marriage," he begged. "What I'm trying to say is that you are special to me. I care about you, and I don't want you to agree to an arrangement you may come to regret."

"There's only one thing that needs to be resolved, Clay. Do you want me, or don't you?"

XX+

Dear Reader,

Happy Valentine's Day! We couldn't send you flowers or chocolate hearts, but here are six wonderful new stories that capture all the magic of falling in love.

Clay Rutledge is the *Father in the Middle* in this emotional story from Phyllis Halldorson. This FABULOUS FATHER needed a new nanny for his little girl. But when he hired pretty Tamara Houston, he didn't know his adopted daughter was the child she'd once given up.

Arlene James continues her heartwarming series, THIS SIDE OF HEAVEN, with *The Rogue Who Came to Stay*. When rodeo champ Griff Shaw came home to find Joan Burton and her daughter living in his house, he couldn't turn them out. But did Joan dare share a roof with this rugged rogue?

There's mischief and romance when two sisters trade places and find love in Carolyn Zane's duet SISTER SWITCH. Meet the first half of this dazzling duo this month in *Unwilling Wife*.

In Patricia Thayer's latest book, Lafe Colter has his heart set on Michelle Royer—the one woman who wants nothing to do with him! Will *The Cowboy's Courtship* end in marriage?

Rounding out the month, Geeta Kingsley brings us *Daddy's Little Girl* and Megan McAllister finds a *Family in the Making* when she moves next door to handsome Sam Armstrong and his adorable kids in a new book by Dani Criss.

Look for more great books in the coming months from favorite authors like Diana Palmer, Elizabeth August, Suzanne Carey and many more.

Happy Reading!

Anne Canadeo
Senior Editor
Silhouette Books

Please address questions and book requests to:
Silhouette Reader Service
U.S.: 3010 Walden Ave., P.O. Box 1325, Buffalo, NY 14269
Canadian: P.O. Box 609, Fort Erie, Ont. L2A 5X3

FATHER IN
THE MIDDLE

Phyllis Halldorson

Silhouette

R O M A N C E™

Published by Silhouette Books

America's Publisher of Contemporary Romance

In loving memory of Robert Kelly,
my own Fabulous Father

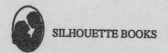

SILHOUETTE BOOKS

ISBN 0-373-19060-3

FATHER IN THE MIDDLE

Copyright © 1995 by Phyllis Halldorson

This edition published by arrangement with Harlequin Enterprises B.V.

® and TM are trademarks of Harlequin Enterprises B. V., used under
license. Trademarks indicated with ® are registered in the United States
Patent and Trademark Office, the Canadian Trade Marks Office and in
other countries.

Printed in U.S.A.

Books by Phyllis Halldorson

PHYLLIS HALLDORSON,

at age sixteen, met her real-life Prince Charming. She married him a year later, and they settled down to raise a family. A compulsive reader, Phyllis dreamed of someday finding the time to write stories of her own. That time came when her two youngest children reached adolescence. When she was introduced to romance novels, she knew she had found her long-delayed vocation. After all, how could she write anything else after living all those years with her very own Silhouette hero?

Clayton Rutledge on Fatherhood...

When my late wife, Alicia, and I were told that we'd never be able to conceive a child together I was disappointed, but I could accept it. I had all I needed to make me happy: a wife I dearly loved, a rewarding profession, and a fine home. But Alicia was crushed, and since it meant so much to her I agreed to adopt.

I wasn't prepared for the jolt that rocked me when that pink bundle was placed in my arms. She was so small! I'd held babies before, but never ones as young or as little. I adjusted the blanket and saw that her blue eyes were open and gazing squarely into mine. I blinked, and she smiled at me. People tell me that's impossible, but what do they know. I put my finger against her tiny hand and she closed her fist around it. A warm flood of love washed through me, and I was hooked. From that instant she was my daughter, our daughter, the child of our love as surely as if she'd been born to me.

Six years later I am a widower and my daughter is the center of my world. Now we have Tamara, who is filling the void in my little girl's life. Can she soothe the ache in my heart, too?

Chapter One

Tamara's three-inch heels, which raised her height to a fairly respectable five feet three inches, tapped noisily as she walked down the uncarpeted hall, then stopped at the door marked Paul Wallace, Private Investigator.

She swallowed and unclenched her fists to flex her fingers in an effort to relax. It wasn't as if she'd impulsively decided on the course of action she was about to take without giving it a lot of serious thought. She'd had years to think about it and weeks to agonizingly debate the pros and cons of her decision. She wasn't going to change her mind now.

Clamping her hand around the doorknob, she turned it and walked into a small reception room. It was clean but far from luxurious. A battered desk took up most of the space, and the window behind it was covered with cream-colored metal blinds but no sheer curtains or drapes to soften the effect. A file cabinet and a brown vinyl-covered sofa were the only other items of furniture, but even so, the room was crowded.

A middle-aged woman behind the desk looked away from her computer screen and adjusted her glasses. "Yes, may I help you?"

Tamara walked the few steps to the desk. "I'm Tamara Houston. I have an appointment with Mr. Wallace at ten o'clock."

The woman nodded toward the door in the wall nearest her. "You can go on in," she said curtly and returned her attention to the computer.

Tamara grimaced and suspected that she should have consulted more than the Yellow Pages in the phone book before selecting a private investigator. On the other hand, they were expensive, and she'd be lucky if she could afford even this one.

She knocked lightly on the door, then opened it. The man sitting behind the desk stood up and smiled as he put out his hand. "Good morning," he said. "I'm Paul Wallace. You're Tamara Houston?"

She put her hand in his, and his clasp was firm and friendly. "How do you do," she answered. "Yes, I'm Tamara."

Once they were seated he got right to the point. "Suppose you tell me what it is you want me to do for you."

His voice had a vibrant timbre that was soothing as well as pleasing, and she decided to put her trust in him after all, in spite of his abominable choice of receptionist and office furniture. He was fiftyish, rotund and balding, not exactly the Magnum, P.I.-type, but she wasn't looking for a lover. There was an air of warmth and reliability about him that inspired confidence, and besides, she was afraid if she didn't do this now she never would.

She took a deep breath and plunged ahead. "I want you to find the baby I gave up for adoption seven years ago."

Paul Wallace's smile disappeared and was replaced by a startled expression. "You couldn't have been more than eleven or twelve years old seven years ago," he said as his gaze roamed over her.

"I was seventeen," she corrected him. "I'm twenty-four now."

He shrugged. "Sorry," he said, "but you don't look more than seventeen now. It doesn't matter, though, because I don't handle that type of investigation." His tone had lost its cordiality and was cool and clipped. "If you'd like, I can recommend an operative who does."

Tamara was taken aback. "But you don't understand—"

"No, I don't," he agreed. "That's why I don't do adoption searches. I can't be unbiased. My wife and I have an adopted child, and we would bitterly resent his birth mother suddenly appearing out of nowhere to reclaim him."

"No! You've got it all wrong." Somehow Tamara had to make him understand. "I've no intention of trying to get my baby back. I just want to see her. To know she's well cared for and loved."

Paul shook his head. "You may have convinced yourself that's all you want, but once you've located her..." He looked at Tamara. "You did say 'her' didn't you?"

She nodded. "Yes. A little girl. She's seven years old now, and I've never seen her. Never held her in my arms—" She choked on a sob.

"Please, don't do this," he interrupted. "Don't put yourself through this because it won't make any difference. I'm on the other side. I'm not going to help you disrupt the lives of a family because years after the fact you decided you didn't want to give up your baby after all."

"But it wasn't like that," she insisted. "I didn't place my daughter for adoption voluntarily. I was forced to give her up."

Paul glared at her. "Oh, come on now, I'm not a lawyer, but I know a lot about adoption law. No woman can be forced to place a newborn child for adoption against her will. It's against the law."

"Someone should have told that to my parents," she responded bitterly. She knew he was right about the emotional damage her appearance after all this time could do to her child and its adoptive parents, but it was important to her that he be made aware of why she had to pursue it anyway. "Please, Mr. Wallace, won't you at least listen to my story? I'll pay for your time, and then, if you still don't want to take the case, I'll let you recommend someone else."

He sighed and his expression softened somewhat. "My name's Paul," he said. "May I call you Tamara?"

"Please do."

"All right, Tamara, if you feel the need to talk I'll listen, and there's no charge, but it's unlikely that you'll change my mind." He leaned back and relaxed. "Now, start at the beginning and tell me what happened."

Tamara tried to follow his example and relax, too, but the rush of memories she was dredging up was too strong and too painful. Instead she straightened her shoulders and leaned forward in her eagerness to impress upon him her desperate need to see her little girl. "I really do need to start at the beginning," she said slowly. "Not just the beginning of the adoption experience, but the beginning of my life."

Paul raised an eyebrow but said nothing as she continued. "I was what you'd call a late baby, born when my mother was forty-one and my father forty-six. They'd been married for ten childless years and were both well established in the business and social communities of the small town in rural Iowa where they lived. My unexpected appearance was definitely a mixed blessing."

Paul chuckled. "I can imagine. You probably shook 'em up real good."

Tamara smiled. "You've got that right. Dad was president of one of the two local banks, and Mother was the secretary at one of the three churches. They weren't at all child oriented and tended to be more uptight and strict than the younger parents of my friends. They lived by the stern, small-town moral code that most of the residents professed but didn't always adhere to. That's why they were so unyielding when..." The lump in Tamara's throat made it difficult for her to go on, and she blinked back the tears she felt pressing behind her eyes.

Paul came to her rescue. "They weren't very supportive when you told them you were pregnant?"

Tamara's nervous giggle was anything but mirthful. "You could say that, yes. They weren't supportive at all. They were furious and promised that I'd go to hell for my 'sin.'" She lowered her glance. "What they didn't tell me was that I wouldn't have to wait until I died for that prediction to come true."

Paul straightened up. "I don't suppose they ever taught you about birth control?"

She shook her head vigorously. "Sex was never mentioned in our home. What little I knew I learned from girlfriends who weren't much better informed. But it wouldn't have done any good if I'd been an expert on the subject...." Again her voice failed, and her eyes burned with unshed tears.

"Just take your time, Tamara, and tell me what happened." Paul's tone was gentle and not at all judgmental.

She pressed her lips together in an effort to stop them from trembling. "It was the night of the high school's annual Thanksgiving ball. I was seldom allowed to date, but this was a special occasion and I'd gone with the captain of the football team. When the dance was over, he drove to the wooded area outside of town that was the teenagers' favorite parking place.

"I'd never been there before, and I knew my parents would be mad if I didn't go right home. I told my date, but he just laughed and put his arms around me. He started to feel me up and I—I struggled, but the more I resisted the more insistent he got, until finally he...he..." The sobs she'd been holding back finally broke loose and shook her.

Tears came pouring out, and she put her face in her hands as she cried.

Paul pushed a box of tissues across the desk, then stood and came around to pat her on the shoulder. "Go ahead and cry, honey. Get it all out. I'll be in the outer office. Just come get me when you're ready to go on."

He left, and Tamara wept. She'd never been able to talk about this with anybody before, and it was like a dam overflowing its gates. She cried for the pain she'd endured during her first and only intercourse, for her shattered innocence, for the baby she'd given up and for the shame she'd endured at the hands of her parents.

It took a long time, but she finally managed to pull herself together and quiet the emotional storm that left her drained but also cleansed. After a trip to the rest room at the end of the hall, where she did what she could to repair her ravaged face, she and Paul returned to his office.

They sat across the desk from each other once more, and he looked at her with a compassion he didn't try to hide. "That bastard raped you, didn't he?"

"Yes, he did," she said emphatically, "but according to my parents' way of thinking, there is no such thing as date rape. If a man forces himself on the woman he's dating, then she must have led him on and only got what she asked for. The fact that I wasn't a woman but a sixteen-year-old girl didn't make any difference, either. Nice girls didn't get pregnant, so I was a two-time slut."

Paul muttered an oath. "How can parents, who were once young themselves, be so blind on the subject of teenage sex?"

Tamara flexed her aching shoulder muscles and settled back in her chair. "How old is your son?"

"Twelve," Paul said. "I've already had the father-son talk with him, and encouraged him to come to me with any questions he has. I just hope to God that I don't blow it when he does."

She smiled. "You won't. I only wish my father had been more like you, but he was as puritanical as my mother. They laid down the law together. I would not be allowed to bring shame on their good name. No one was to know of my condition. Abortion was out of the question since their religious beliefs discouraged it, but I would be sent away to have my baby, and it would be given up for adoption at birth."

"And you went along with their demands?"

She nodded. "I had to. It broke my heart, but without support from my parents, which they adamantly refused to give if I kept the baby, I had no way to care for it. I was shipped off to Fort Worth, Texas, to a private home for pregnant girls who wanted to give up their babies for adoption. I completed the second semester of my junior year there." Her voice quivered and she took a deep breath. "The baby was born on August 30. I never saw her except for a fleeting glimpse as they whisked her out of the delivery room. A week later, I returned home to Iowa and started my senior year of school."

"And your parents?" Paul inquired. "What was your relationship with them after—"

"We were like strangers living in the same house, polite but distant. I applied for and was accepted at the University of Iowa. As soon as I graduated from high school, I came to Ames and found a part-time job. I got my B.A. in education two years ago and have been teaching second grade in an elementary school here since then.

"My parents paid for my college education, but we don't keep in touch. I haven't been back to my hometown since I left there six years ago."

Paul tapped the desk with a pencil. "It's sad to think that an interlude in the back seat of a car can so drastically alter the course of three lives," he observed thoughtfully. "Four, actually, if you count the baby who never should have been conceived."

"Yes, it is sad," Tamara agreed, "and that's the point I'm trying to make. My life was totally disrupted, and believe me, that's not something I'd deliberately inflict on anybody else. Certainly not my own child. But don't you see? I feel responsible for her. I conceived her, gave birth to her, then signed her over to strangers to raise."

Paul opened his mouth to say something, but she held up her hand. "No, please, let me finish. I'm haunted by the possibility that her adoptive parents may be abusing her—"

"Tamara!" This time, Paul didn't give her a chance to hush him. "That's most unlikely. The social services—"

"The social services don't check on the parties once the adoption is completed," Tamara reminded him. "I know this is a sore subject with you, and I don't want you to think that I'm suggesting you and your wife have been anything but exemplary parents to your adopted son, but I have to know that my child is loved and well treated, too. I owe her that much, and I'll never be able to make peace with the fact that I gave her up, no matter how unwillingly, until I've investigated for myself."

He looked uncertain. "I understand how you feel, but what do you plan to do once you've found her?"

"Paul, I swear that I'm not going to intrude into her life if she's happy, healthy and well adjusted. I'll find some way to see her without either her or her adoptive parents knowing who I am. I'm a teacher. I work with children her age every day, and I know the difference between strictness and abuse. If everything's all right, I'll come right back here and get on with my own life."

He put down the pencil he'd been tapping. "You say that now, but how can I be sure you'll do it once you see her?"

Tamara shook her head sadly. "You can't. You'll just have to trust me." She held out her hands, palms up in supplication. "Please help me. You can find her. I know you can." Her voice broke, and she hated behaving so emotionally, but she couldn't help it. Her self-control had been washed away with the tears, and she was subsisting on raw nerves.

Paul hesitated for a long time, and her apprehension escalated in proportion until she was about to scream. He finally said, "All right, I'll make an exception in your case, but I'm warning you. If you do anything to upset that family needlessly, I'll—"

If he finished the sentence she didn't hear it above the massive sob that shook her, as for the second time in the last hour, she broke down and wept.

A week went by, and Tamara spent the better part of it pacing in front of the telephone although Paul had warned her that these things take time. She chided herself for not putting this search in motion before school had let out for the summer. At least then she'd have had something else to keep her busy.

Finally, on the eighth day, the phone rang and this time it was Paul. "I have good news," he said cheerfully. "I've found the child." Tamara was ecstatic, but he refused to tell her anything else over the phone. "Come in at one-thirty this afternoon and I'll give you the full report," he commanded.

She was at his office by one o'clock and had to wait outside the locked door until he and the receptionist came back from lunch. He ushered her into the inner office and when they were both seated he opened a folder on his desk.

"Your baby was adopted by a couple in San Antonio. Clayton and Alicia Rutledge," he began. "He's a dentist, an oral surgeon, and she's an architect. They live in the King William section of San Antonio, an area of huge old homes, called castles by many, which have been restored and are now historical treasures."

Tamara was bubbling over with excitement and questions. "Is she well? What did they name her? Have you seen her?'' The questions were coming into her mind faster than she could ask them, and she didn't allow any time for answers.

Paul laughed and held up both hands. "Whoa, there. Slow down and give me a chance. The little girl's name is Mary Frances, and as far as I could ascertain she's perfectly healthy. You told me your finances were limited and you couldn't afford to spend much, so I've kept the cost down by working from records only. If you want me to go to Texas and check all this out in person, it will be a lot more expensive.''

Tamara was shaking with excitement. "Oh, thanks, but that won't be necessary." Her voice vibrated with happiness. "I'll take over from now on. Is there anything else about her that you can tell me?"

"Only that she attends a private school. I'll give you the name and address. Oh, and I also checked with the state dental association and learned that Dr. Rutledge is one of the best known and most respected dental surgeons in Texas." Paul paused and looked at her. "Now I've held up my part of the bargain, and I expect you to hold up yours. What do you plan to do with this information I've given you?"

Tamara's head was spinning, and she could hardly talk, let alone think. "Do? I'm going to San Antonio, of course."

He frowned. "And then what?"

"I'm going to see my little girl, make sure she's okay." What was the matter with Paul anyway? He knew what she'd planned to do once she'd found her child.

"She's not your little girl anymore, Tamara, and there's no need for you to see her. I've found out that her adoptive parents are professional people, well respected in the community, and financially stable enough to live in an upscale section of town and send her to a private school. What more do you need to know?"

His obvious disapproval of her plans took some of the edge off her excitement and she resented it. "I do need to see her! Darn it, Paul, I've already told you that. I have an overwhelming need to see my daughter, and neither you nor anyone else is going to stop me."

He stood and leaned over the desk glowering at her. "You told me that you wanted to make sure she was well cared for and loved. Well, I've just proven to you that she is, so there's no reason for you to go down there and see her. Leave her alone, Tamara! Don't interfere in her life at this late date."

He was finally getting through the fog of pure joy that held her enthralled, and she didn't like what she was hearing. She, too, stood and faced him, although since she hadn't taken the time to change from her jeans and flat-heeled shoes she had to look up nearly a foot to do it. "All you've proved to me is that she lives in San Antonio and has well-to-do adoptive parents." She heard the irritation in her tone and regretted it, but she wasn't going to let him ruin her jubilation. "That certainly doesn't guarantee that she's well treated and happy. I promised you that I wouldn't make myself known to the Rutledges unless Mary Frances was being mistreated, and I'll honor that promise, but I have to see the child I gave birth to if only for a few minutes. I have to know that the Rutledges love her and treat her well."

Paul glared at her for a few more seconds, then sank wearily back into his chair. "I just hope to God I haven't opened a Pandora's box that I can't control," he muttered and wiped his hand over his face.

Chapter Two

It was late afternoon when Tamara turned her blue compact car off the highway and into the heart of downtown San Antonio. She'd been driving steadily from dawn until dark for two long days and she was exhausted, but even so, her excitement hadn't abated.

Tomorrow she'd see her child. The baby she'd carried inside her body for nine months. The daughter who called someone else mother. Her triumph over fate was bittersweet. She could never claim the youngster. She knew that, but from now on for the rest of her life she'd know who her child was, where she was, and how to find her when the need to see her again became too great to resist.

Tamara had never been to San Antonio before, but her travel agent had given her maps. She had the route marked and memorized on the city map from the freeway to the King William section of town. The agency had also provided her with a list of hotels, motels and inns, and she'd made reservations at one of the many "castles" in the area that had been turned into bed-and-breakfast lodgings. She'd intended to go there first and get a good night's sleep before looking for the Rutledge home, but, as if they had a mind of their own, her hands turned the steering wheel at the right corner and headed for that house instead.

As she drove slowly looking for streets and numbers, she could see why the edifices had been dubbed castles. The lovely old homes, although certainly not of castle dimensions, were huge by today's standards and predominantly Gothic and Italianate in style. Built of stone, wood and brick, they were set in the middle of oversize lots shaded by ancient live oak and crepe myrtle trees.

Tamara was pleased to know that her daughter lived in this affluent old historical area of town. Money didn't guarantee happiness, but people who had it were seldom deprived of any of the necessities or comforts of life.

It only took a few minutes to find the street she was looking for, and the third house from the corner was marked with the right numbers. This two-story, asymmetrical home built of limestone was true Gothic architecture. Its gabled roof and diamond-paned windows shaped in pointed arches were trimmed with fanciful decorative ornamentation cut from wood.

She noted that the wide front door was intricately carved from heavy oak and that a waist-high white picket fence enclosed the front half of the lot. This was replaced by a high stone wall that totally hid the back of the property from sight—no doubt a security measure since it looked much newer than the picket fence.

Tamara drove past the house to the end of the block, then turned around and came back to park across the street, where she could look at it without being obvious. There were no cars in the long driveway, but there was a detached garage outside the wall on the left side that would hold at least two vehicles. If the family was at home their cars were probably in there.

She sat watching and getting the feel of the area for some time, but there was no sign of the occupants and Tamara's muscles were aching from the long confinement and stress of her trip. Eventually she realized she'd better find her bed-and-breakfast inn and register before they rented her room to someone else.

She found the inn only a few blocks from the Rutledge place. There was no sign or other indication that it was a former residence converted to commercial property. It looked like any other home in the area. A three-story wooden structure with a wraparound porch, it was painted white with gray trim. The interior was furnished with lovely antiques, and she was given a room on the second floor overlooking the back gardens. She didn't have a private bath, but there were two shared ones at either end of the hall.

She declined the innkeeper's invitation to join the other guests downstairs in the living room for coffee, tea or wine. Instead she took a bubble bath and climbed into her canopied bed where she fell asleep almost immediately.

Tamara awoke the next morning feeling refreshed and eager to get on with her quest. As she buttoned up a red coatdress, which she hoped made her look like a grown-up instead of the teenager she was usually taken for, she fine-tuned the plan she'd been orchestrating on her drive down from Ames.

After a buffet breakfast in the dining room, where even the pastry was home baked, she asked the innkeeper if the schools had been let out yet for the summer. Much to her delight, she was told that they would be open for one more week before vacation started.

Using her city map again, she found The Mission Trail Academy, the private school little Mary Frances attended. Since it wasn't a parochial school, Tamara assumed that it was so named because it was situated in the Mission Trail section of the city, where four of San Antonio's five restored missions were located. The school was a sprawling modern building with lots of glass and walkways, and a large playground. Tamara's heart pounded and her knees were wobbly as she got out of the car.

She would see her long-lost daughter in a matter of minutes.

Taking a deep, steadying breath, she opened the school door and went inside. In the office she identified herself as a vacationing teacher and asked to see the principal. Luck was with her, and she was ushered into an inner office and introduced to a pleasant middle-aged woman named Mrs. Oxenberg.

"How do you do, Ms. Houston," the principal said from behind her desk. "Please, sit down. How may I help you?"

Tamara lowered herself into the chair at the front of the desk and smiled. "I teach second grade in the public school system in Ames, Iowa, and am also studying for my master's degree. I'm writing my thesis on some of the new techniques and curricula that private schools in different parts of the country are using, so I'm taking advantage of my vacation this summer to do some traveling and research at the same time."

"What a marvelous idea," Mrs. Oxenberg said, "using your summer break to work on your advanced degree. I congratulate you on being so dedicated to your profession."

Tamara squirmed uncomfortably. Although she did plan to get her master's eventually, she hadn't started back to school yet. She hated lying to this nice woman, but it was the only way she could think of to get permission to observe Mary Frances Rutledge's second-grade classroom.

Pushing her guilty conscience aside, she continued, "Oh, thank you, but I'm enjoying every minute of it. It would be a great help if you'd give me permission to speak with your second-grade teacher and observe her classroom methods. I promise I won't intrude or disrupt the class in any way."

Tamara held her breath as Mrs. Oxenberg hesitated for some time before answering. "I'll have to see your identification first. A necessary precaution, you know, but if it's in order I don't see why not. Provided the teacher agrees, of course. Did you want to do this now?"

Tamara sagged with relief. "Yes, if it could be arranged. I know it's short notice, but..." She rummaged in her purse and handed the woman her driver's license plus the teaching credentials she'd remembered to bring.

Mrs. Oxenberg examined the documents and handed them back. "If you'll wait here, I'll talk to the teacher," she said and left the room. She was back in a few minutes with the good news that the teacher had agreed, and led Tamara down the hall to a bright and sunny classroom at the back of the building.

She was shaking with excitement, but when they got to the room it was empty except for the teacher, a pretty young woman about Tamara's age, who was introduced as Jenny Lou Perry. "Call me J.L.," she said with a teasing grimace. "My mother had a propensity for double names. My sisters are Mary Ellen, Beth Ann and Billee Jo." She laughed. "Billee Jo is the youngest, and she was supposed to be a boy."

Tamara laughed with her, and it relieved some of the strain.

"The kids are at recess," J.L. explained, "but they'll be back in a few minutes. You want to observe my class?"

Tamara nodded and told her the same story she'd told the principal. "I promise not to be a nuisance," she concluded. "I'll just sit in a corner and the children will forget I'm even there."

"Oh no, you're not getting off that easy," J.L. said with a laugh. "I expect you to do your share of the teaching."

Just then the bell sounded, and seconds later the building rang with the noise of dozens of small feet pounding down the concrete halls. Before Tamara had a chance to get

nto another dither, a group of children trooped into the
oom and sat down at their desks.

She scanned them quickly. Twelve girls and nine boys.
The girls were all dressed alike in blue plaid pleated skirts
nd white blouses while the boys wore dark slacks and white
hirts. A small class compared to her group of thirty in the
ublic school. She envied J.L. the extra time she had to
pend with each child.

Which one of the girls was Mary Frances? Four of them
vere Afro-American and two were Oriental, so that nar-
owed her choices. Would she be able to pick her daughter
ut of the others?

Before she could concentrate on them individually, the
eacher clapped her hands for their attention. "Class," she
aid as they grudgingly quieted down. "We have a visitor."
he looked toward Tamara and motioned her to stand up.
"This is Miss Houston. She's a teacher in the state of Iowa.
Can any of you show us on the map where Iowa is?"

One of the girls, a blonde with blue eyes, raised her hand,
nd Tamara tensed. Could this be her child? But neither she
lor the baby's father had blue eyes.

"All right, Cassandra, let's see if you know."

Cassandra. Wrong name. Obviously that child wasn't
lers.

By the time Tamara focused her attention again, the lit-
le girl had pointed out Iowa on the large map of the United
States hanging on the wall, and returned to her seat.

"That's very good, Cassandra," J.L. said, "and in a few
ninutes Miss Houston will tell you all about Iowa, but now
want you each to stand up and tell her your name. We'll
tart with Ricardo." She nodded to the dark-haired His-
panic boy who sat in the first chair of the first row.

He stood and Tamara's stomach muscles clenched as her
leartbeat accelerated. *In a matter of seconds she was going
o learn which one of these little girls was her daughter.*

As each girl stood, Tamara's breath caught and her head spun. By the time they got to the third row she could feel perspiration dripping down her body. Then, in the middle of that row, a dark-haired little girl rose to her feet. She was smaller than the others, with a delicate bone structure, a creamy complexion and big, round brown eyes that were an exact replica of Tamara's. "My name is Francie Rutledge," she said and sat down again.

Tamara's vision blurred, and for a minute she was afraid she was either going to faint or be sick, but as the children's voices droned on she managed to pull herself together. It was crucial that she not betray her emotional state. If she broke down she'd ruin everything. The school authorities wouldn't take kindly to her lying to them to gain admittance, and if they found out the truth—that she was searching for the Rutledges' adopted child—they'd have her arrested.

Tamara forced herself to drag her hungry gaze away from little Francie, as she called herself, and concentrate on the task at hand. The teacher wanted her to talk to the children about Iowa. It could be disastrous if she flubbed it.

The two hours until lunch seemed to fly by. At J.L.'s request, Tamara acted as a teacher's assistant and worked directly with the children. It was a heady experience. She was able to call on Francie to answer questions or recite something, but she had to be careful not to single the child out for too much attention.

Tamara ached to put her arms around the little girl and hold her, or even just run her hands lovingly through the silky black hair that was the same color as her own. Somehow she kept her distance and contented herself with the sight of her and the sound of her sweet young voice with the slight Texas accent.

When the bell rang for lunch break, Tamara longed to join the children in the cafeteria and talk to Francie while she ate, but her pass was up at noon and she didn't dare ask for an extension. Instead she thanked the children as a group for allowing her to spend the morning with them, then said goodbye to J.L. and Mrs. Oxenberg and left knowing that she hadn't seen the last of her little girl quite yet.

Tamara drove back to the inn and used the phone in the library to call Dr. Clayton Rutledge's dental office. Her hands shook as she listened to the ring at the other end of the line. It went on and on before it finally occurred to her that the office was probably closed for lunch. Damn, she should have thought of that.

She was about to hang up when there was a click and a breathless voice answered, "Dr. Rutledge's office."

Tamara sighed with relief. "This is Tamara Houston," she said as she went over in her mind the story she'd decided on. "I'm vacationing in San Antonio, and I have a toothache. I'd like to make an appointment to see Dr. Rutledge as soon as possible."

"I'm sorry," the voice said, "but Dr. Rutledge is an oral surgeon, and we work only by referrals. If you'd like, I can give you the number of the local dental association—"

Tamara's heart sank, but she wasn't going to give up. "No, you don't understand. The tooth that hurts is a partially impacted wisdom tooth that my dentist back home tells me should be pulled, but it will have to be done by an oral surgeon." That much was true except that the tooth didn't hurt.

"Well...I..." The receptionist didn't sound encouraging.

"I'm a teacher," Tamara hurried to explain, "and I was working as an assistant this morning in the second-grade class at The Mission Trail Academy. I mentioned the toothache to one of the adults there. She said Francie Rutledge's father was a dentist and he might be able to work me in."

"Oh. You know the doctor's daughter?"

"Well, not really," Tamara admitted, "but she was one of the students I worked with. A beautiful child, and bright, too. I'd appreciate it if he would see me. If I can't get it taken care of by tomorrow, I'll have to suffer over the whole weekend...." She let her voice trail off and hoped the woman was compassionate.

There was a moment of silence before the answer came. "I do have a cancellation tomorrow morning at ten o'clock. We have regular patients waiting, but if yours is an emergency—"

"Oh, please," Tamara interrupted, "I'll be ever so grateful. It's really very painful."

Again the receptionist hesitated, but when she spoke, her tone was firm. "All right, Ms. Houston, we wouldn't want your vacation in our city ruined by a toothache. If you can be here by ten tomorrow—"

"Oh, yes, of course I can." Tamara was babbling, but she couldn't help it. This appointment with her daughter's adoptive father was crucial to her. She thanked the receptionist several times and finally hung up.

Tamara rose early the next morning and after breakfast drove over to the Rutledge home, where she again parked across the street and waited. She was hoping to catch a glimpse of the child and her parents when she left for school.

At seven-thirty her patience was rewarded when an unmarked bus drove up in front of the house, and Francie came out escorted by a large, plain-looking woman wearing slacks and an oversize striped cotton shirt. Surely that wasn't Alicia Rutledge. For one thing she was too old. She had to be at least in her late fifties.

The woman walked to the van with the little girl and stood there until Francie was aboard and seated. The door slid shut and the van pulled away from the curb. Only then did the woman turn and go back into the house.

So Mission Trail Academy bused their students to school. The woman was probably an employee who looked after Francie while her parents worked.

A short time later, the garage door opened and a shiny black Cadillac backed down the driveway and sped away. The windows were darkened and Tamara couldn't see who was in it.

Tamara arrived at the dental office ahead of time, but even so, the waiting room was full. When she checked in at the window, she was told that the doctor had had an emergency earlier and they were now running late.

The receptionist gave her a clipboard with a personal and medical information form and told her to fill it out. After she'd answered all the questions, she handed it back, then returned to her seat to wait.

She wondered if she really had sinned as her mother had said and was being punished by all these interminable delays. At this rate, her nervous system was going to wear out long before the rest of her. Although she'd finally seen her daughter, the suspense had built up again when she'd made the appointment to meet her child's adoptive father. Once more she waited while her nerve endings screamed.

After about ten minutes, another patient was called into the operatory. As she glanced around the room at the number of people still waiting, she decided to put the time to good use by finding out all she could about the dentist. She focused on the elderly woman to her left who had smiled at her when she sat down. Tamara leaned over and murmured, "Excuse me, but I was wondering...that is, has Dr. Rutledge treated you before."

The woman smiled again. "Oh my, yes. I've had a lot of work done lately. It's such a bother, but better than dentures."

"This is my first time here, and I'm a little nervous," Tamara said anxiously. "Is he good? I mean, he won't hurt me, will he?"

"Oh, no, he's very gentle," the woman assured her. "I know he's more careful than most because last year he took a month off when his wife died and I had to go to another dentist...."

Tamara was stunned. *His wife died!* But when? How? How did Paul Wallace miss that in his report?

But, of course, Paul hadn't been looking for death notices.

The woman droned on, but Tamara didn't hear what she was saying. So Mary Frances didn't have a mother after all. How had this affected her? How had it affected her father? Would he know how to take care of a little girl?

The sound of the door opening and the dental assistant summoning another patient jolted Tamara's attention back to the woman beside her. She had quit talking and was looking at Tamara rather strangely. "I'm sorry," Tamara said. "I'm afraid my mind was wandering. Did you say that Dr. Rutledge is a widower?"

The woman nodded. "Yes, such a tragedy. It was in the papers and on television. She was a Conrad, you know. Her family was one of the early settlers of the King William area of town. They made their money in milling. You've probably heard of the Conrad Flour Mills—"

"But what happened to her?" Tamara cried, trying to keep the impatience out of her voice. After all, the poor woman couldn't know how important this was to her.

"It was an accident. She was an architect, you see, and was on the site where one of her buildings was going up. I don't know exactly what happened, but the crane malfunctioned somehow and hit her. She only lived for a few hours after they took her to the hospital."

Tamara shuddered. Dear God, how awful.

"I understand the doctor was inconsolable," the woman continued. "He didn't come back to his office for over a month, and even now he looks so sad. He used to laugh and joke with his patients, but not anymore. Oh, he's always friendly, but you can tell that he's still grieving."

Tamara felt a wave of compassion for the man, but her first thought was for her daughter. "Does he have any children?" she asked as a means of inquiring about Francie.

"Just one, a little girl. She's a beautiful child."

Tamara's eyes widened. "Do you know her?"

The woman shook her head. "Well, no, I've never seen her in person, but he's got her pictures in all of the operatories. Updates them every few months. It's obvious that he adores her."

Before Tamara could comment, the door opened again, and when the assistant called a name the woman said, "That's me," then got up and followed her inside.

Tamara fidgeted for another half hour before she was finally called and taken into one of the operatories. Her informant had been right. There were several framed pictures of Mary Frances in different poses arranged on one wall. Tamara would have given everything she owned to have just one of them.

The assistant seated her in the full-length chair. "I understand you're an emergency patient," she said. "Is the tooth still bothering you?"

Tamara certainly didn't want to have the tooth pulled if she didn't have to, so she admitted that it wasn't. "I must have just bit down wrong on something," she said, and the embarrassment in her tone was real. "I feel so silly after making such a fuss about getting an appointment with the doctor, but since I'm here I'd like for him to look at it anyway. It could even be cracked."

The assistant looked annoyed, but she only commented, "Then we'll still have to take X rays," before covering her with a protective shield and stuffing hard-edged film in her mouth.

When that unpleasant procedure was over, the assistant substituted a large plastic bib for the shield and lowered the chair so Tamara was lying nearly flat, then announced that the doctor would be with her in a few minutes and left. Oh, no, not more delay! She actually groaned aloud at the prospect of still another long stretch of nervous anticipation before a male voice from behind made her jump.

"Are you in pain? I understood Blanche to say your toothache was gone."

Tamara's gaze flew upward and connected with a pair of warm golden brown eyes set in a face that was handsomer than most, and had probably been boyish before it was marked by tragedy. Now there were lines of suffering stamped around his eyes and mouth, and although she knew he was only in his late thirties, his black hair had wings of white at the temples.

She felt a rush of compassion for him, and it had nothing to do with the fact that he was now her daughter's father. He was a man in pain, and she had an almost irresistible urge to reach out and caress his ravaged but still good-looking face.

She fought back the tide of emotion that had taken her totally by surprise. This was absurd. He was a stranger. Her only interest in him was his connection to her baby. Swallowing, she hoped she still had a voice. "No...I mean, yes..." Oh, great! She was behaving like a lovestruck movie-star fan. She gulped and tried again. "I'm sorry. I mean no, I'm not in pain, and yes, the toothache is gone."

He smiled, and she nearly melted. It was a warm smile but it didn't erase the sadness in his eyes.

"I'm the one who's sorry," he said kindly. "I usually try to meet new patients while they're still on their feet before they get stuck in that chair, but today we're simply swamped. I'm Dr. Rutledge, and according to your chart, you're...Tamara Houston?" As he looked at her, his expression changed from friendly to puzzled. "Have I treated you before? You look familiar."

His voice was a smooth baritone that sent ripples up her spine, but his question alarmed her. Was he seeing Francie in her? They did look a lot alike.

"No, I've never been in San Antonio before," she hastened to assure him. "I've lived all my life in Iowa, and am just here on vacation. I'm afraid I intimidated your receptionist into giving me an appointment, and then the pain went away."

He picked up a pair of latex surgical gloves and pulled them on. "Well, we'll take a look and see if there's a problem. So did you just pick me out of the phone book?"

It took a few seconds to get her thoughts unscrambled before she answered. "Oh, no, I'm a teacher. I was visiting your daughter's school yesterday as part of a research project I'm working on, and it was someone there who recommended you."

He didn't look surprised, just nodded and said, "Open your mouth," then put his fingers in it when she did. "Francie told me they had a teacher's assistant yesterday morning," he said. "Will you be in San Antonio long?" He took his fingers out of her mouth and turned slightly to pick up some instruments from a tray.

"Not nearly as long as I'd like to be," she said, and meant every word. "It's a wonderful old city, and I'd spend the whole summer here if I could get a temporary job."

Again he told her to open her mouth, then examined it with the instruments. "I'm desperately looking for a housekeeper in case you're interested in applying," he told her jokingly.

Tamara was dumbfounded. Dear Lord, if he was serious he'd just opened the way for her to help raise her daughter, at least temporarily. If she played her cards right, she might even be able to convince him to extend it to a permanent position.

Fortunately her mouth was too full of hardware to talk. It forced her to think first. She mustn't sound too eager. It was best to play it cool, to lightly banter the subject about for a while before she let him know she was interested in the position.

"Hey, I just might take you up on that," she said as lightly as she could manage when he took the tools out of her mouth. "It sounds like the perfect summertime employment."

He looked a little surprised and chuckled. "Don't be too sure about that. My angelic-looking young daughter can be a little devil when she puts her mind to it."

Tamara laughed. "I don't believe that for a minute. I've never encountered a more polite child."

He nodded solemnly. "Yes, she has good manners. Her mother insisted on that. She always said there was no excuse for a child to be rude, and she taught Francie well."

She caught the sorrow in his tone, and again her hormones flared. But she was gradually regaining her self-control, and when she answered she deliberately used the present tense. "As a teacher I wish there were more mothers like your wife. She's giving her daughter a gift beyond price by teaching her to be gracious to others."

Tamara saw the flicker of pain that crossed his face. "Yes, she was a loving wife and mother, but she...she died last year, and I find it difficult to be stern with Francie. She misses her mother so."

Tamara's sympathy for this man was overwhelming. It was obviously still deeply painful for him to talk about his wife's death. Her first inclination was to comfort him, and it was a difficult one to ignore. Her second was to offer her condolences and then move quickly on to some other subject, but it seemed reasonable to assume that his need for a housekeeper was tied in to the fact that he was a widower and she had to get him back on that subject.

"I'm so sorry," she said, trying to keep her tone unemotional. "It must be difficult for both of you. Is that the reason you need a housekeeper?" She knew she was being pushy, asking questions that were none of her business, but this would be her only opportunity to get the information she wanted.

He nodded tersely. "Partly. Our present one had been with my wife's family for many years, and with us since our marriage, but she's past retirement age, and Alicia's accident was a blow she's not recovering from. Her doctor has strongly advised her to retire and get away from here, live near her daughter and grandchildren in New Mexico."

"That sounds like good advice," Tamara said. "I assume she's taking it?"

Again he told her to open her mouth and poked around inside. "Yes, she's leaving as soon as school's out next week," he answered as he probed. "I hadn't expected it to be so difficult to find a replacement, but I soon found that I'd been living in a fantasy world. Employees like Hertha are almost nonexistent nowadays. She's always been like one of the family. So far, I haven't interviewed anyone I'd trust to be a part-time mother to my daughter."

Tamara was greatly relieved to hear that he was so particular about who he hired to care for Francie. It also might make it easier for her to convince him to give her the job for the summer since she was certainly well qualified. She was a teacher, and she loved children. *Especially Francie.*

When he finally let her close her mouth again she took a deep breath and launched into her pitch. "Dr. Rutledge, I wasn't altogether kidding around when I said I might be interested in the position. I'm fascinated by San Antonio and would love to spend the summer here. I'm free of entanglements, have no husband or family, and while I'm not the world's best cook and housekeeper, I am a teacher with two years' experience in handling children. My record is blemish free."

He looked startled. "Are you serious?"

"Yes, I am. I take temporary jobs in Ames during the summers to supplement my income, but I haven't lined one

up yet. I could stay until you find just the person you're
looking for.''

She crossed her fingers and offered up a fervent, though
unspoken, prayer as the seconds ticked away and her future
was held captive by the ominous silence.

Chapter Three

Tamara was jolted out of her unnerving suspense by an assistant who entered the room and handed Dr. Rutledge an envelope. He stripped off his gloves, nodded a dismissal and opened it. Pulling out the strip of X rays, he turned away from Tamara and put it on the lighted screen, then examined it while she stewed.

Was he just going to ignore her offer and not even answer? Had she made a fatal mistake by applying for the position too soon? Did he think she was some kind of kook who would say or do anything to get a cushy job with a wealthy family in order to steal some of their valuables?

She was about to scream with frustration when he finally turned back to her. "Your X rays don't show a reason for your toothache," he said as if that was their only topic of conversation. "No cavity or abscess, and the tooth isn't cracked, but impacted teeth do cause problems." He reached down and pushed the button that raised her chair to a sitting position. "It probably won't bother you again right away, but I advise you to see your own dentist when you get back home and have it extracted.''

Tamara's heart sank. So he was going to dismiss her without giving her an answer. Now what was she going to do? If she argued or pleaded, it would only reinforce his suspicion that she was a little nutty. While she was still fighting her way out of the mental fog of disappointment and uncertainty he reached out and unfastened the plastic bib, then whisked it away.

"Oh, and about the housekeeping position," he said with a smile. "If you're sure you want it, leave the names, addresses and phone numbers of three references with the receptionist before you leave. I'll check them and get back to you soon."

It's a good thing he rushed away because it wouldn't do for him to see the pure elation that she knew was shining from her face.

Tamara hardly left the inn over the weekend for fear of missing Dr. Rutledge's call. She'd named as references the principal of the school where she taught, the minister of her church and her favorite professor at the university where she'd always been in the top five percent of her classes.

Even so, she worried and cursed the telephone that rang for others but never for her. Until Sunday evening. She was sitting right by the phone in the library and answered it immediately.

It was Clayton Rutledge, and he got right to the point. "I've checked your references and they're excellent. If you're still interested in the position, I'd like you to come to the house for dinner tomorrow night so we can all get to know each other a little better before we make any commitments. Are you free?"

Was she free? Darn right she was, and she told him so, but in a somewhat more formal manner.

The next evening Tamara dressed carefully from the meager supply of clothing she'd brought with her. Although most of her summer dresses and skirts were mid-thigh in length, in the interest of dignity, she chose a lime green chemise with a hem that skimmed her knee. Except that it had a snug bodice that defined the fullness of her high breasts and a scoop neckline that promised but never quite delivered an occasional glimpse of that gentle rise of flesh.

She arrived at the Rutledge home on the dot of seven, the time agreed on. Her stomach was filled with butterflies as she walked up to the front door and rang the bell. She'd be seeing her little girl again and that expectation was uppermost in her mind, but now she was excited about seeing Francie's father again, too. That bothered her.

If it was just because she hoped he'd be her employer for the summer and she wanted to make a good impression, she wouldn't have given it a second thought, but it wasn't. There was something about the man that charmed her, and that was dangerous. She hadn't been seriously attracted to a man since the rape that left her terrified and pregnant.

So what was it about this one that appealed to her so strongly? He was good-looking but not outstandingly so, and he hadn't shown the slightest interest in her except as a patient and possible employee.

Before she could explore the thought further, the door opened and there he stood in front of her. He was dressed in navy slacks and a blue tweed sport coat with a white shirt and blue paisley tie. She'd been wrong. He *was* outstandingly good-looking, in an understated sort of way.

He smiled at her and stepped back. "You're very punctual. Please, come in."

"Thank you," she answered stiffly and walked into a large entry hall that featured a tile floor, a magnificent crystal chandelier and a majestic staircase.

"Dinner will be ready in a few minutes," he said, his tone almost as stiff as hers. Apparently they were both uneasy.

"My daughter, Mary Frances, is waiting in the living room. Shall we join her?"

Her heart pounded at the thought of seeing her child again. "By all means," she consented and followed him into a huge room on their right that was big enough for two furniture groupings without being crowded. Francie stood waiting patiently in front of a magnificent marble fireplace.

She looked like a little princess standing there in a silky rose-colored dress trimmed in lace, with her dark curly hair tumbling around her shoulders. Her delicate face lit up with a smile when Tamara and her father walked into the room. "Hi, Miss Houston," she said happily, moving quickly to meet them. "Daddy said you were coming for dinner. Are you going to teach us at school again?"

Purely by reflex, Tamara hunkered down so that she was eye level with the little girl, who was short for her age just as Tamara had always been. "No, Francie, I'm not. The school in Iowa where I teach is out for the summer and I'm on vacation. I was just visiting your school."

Dr. Rutledge stood beside them. "Why don't you sit down and talk with Francie," he suggested to Tamara, "while I go tell Hertha you're here and she can serve any time."

Feeling a little foolish, Tamara stood and took a seat on the sofa while he walked away. Francie followed her and sat down beside her, giving Tamara a jolt of pure pleasure. It was all she could do not to reach out and hug the child, but she didn't want to appear overeager and frighten or repel her.

"So, Francie," she began as she cast around for something to talk about, "are you glad that school is almost over?"

The little girl screwed up her face. "Yeah, I guess. But I don't want to go to the ranch."

"The ranch?" Tamara asked, startled.

"Grandpa and Grandma's ranch. Daddy says if we don't find a housekeeper by the time school's out, I'll have to spend the summer at the ranch, but I'd rather stay here. There's no one to play with out there."

So that's why her father was so desperate to find a housekeeper. Once his present one was gone, he wouldn't have anyone to look after Francie when she was home all day. Before she could respond, Dr. Rutledge came back, and Francie bounced off the sofa and ran to him. He caught her with his hands spanning her waist and hefted her over his head before sitting down in one of the chairs with her on his lap.

The smile on his face now reached all the way to his eyes. Obviously he loved his little adopted daughter with all his heart. Tamara felt relief and a small lightening of the burden of guilt she carried for giving up her baby.

"Did you tell Miss Houston what happened at school today?" he asked Francie with obvious pride.

"I got all A's on my report card," she announced happily.

Tamara felt a burst of pride, too. "That's great," she told the youngster enthusiastically, "but I'm not at all surprised. I'll bet you get a lot of A's."

"I got one B last time," she said.

Tamara laughed. "Well, no one can be perfect all the time."

She turned her attention to Clayton Rutledge. "I understood school wouldn't be over until later in the week."

He nodded. "That's right, but at Mission Trail report cards are given out a few days earlier to make it easier to handle any problems or surprises the parents may have with the grades." Just then a stout older woman appeared in the doorway to announce that dinner was ready. Dr. Rutledge invited her into the room and he and Tamara stood. "Hertha," he said, "this is Tamara Houston, the young lady I told you about. Tamara, Hertha Gross, my dear friend and housekeeper.''

Tamara was impressed by his sensitivity to this longtime employee, and the two women nodded to each other. ''Pleased to meet you,'' Hertha said rather awkwardly. She was a plain-looking woman with streaks of gray in her brown hair, and a matronly build. She wore a flowered brown silky dress, protected by a full-length apron, and chunky orthopedic shoes.

''And I'm pleased to meet you,'' Tamara replied. ''If you're the one who's cooking dinner, I have to tell you the aroma is making my mouth water.''

Dinner was a pleasant meal of roast beef, potatoes, gravy, asparagus, tossed green salad and ice cream with home-made cookies for dessert. Hertha served, but she also took off her apron and ate with them, and before long the awkwardness of strangers disappeared.

The first thing Dr. Rutledge did was put them all on a first-name basis. ''My name is Clayton,'' he told Tamara, ''but my friends call me Clay. I hope you will, too. May we call you Tamara?''

''Please do,'' she said, and included Francie and Hertha in her gaze. ''I love your home, Clay. You certainly have a lot of room.''

''Too much for us,'' he agreed, ''but it was my late wife's family home. It was built by her great-great-grandfather. He was one of the German merchants who settled this area of town in the late eighteen hundreds. The house has ten-inch-thick limestone exterior walls and the blue roof that was so popular among the German settlers.''

Tamara's eyes widened. ''A blue roof? I didn't notice that. Why were they so popular?''

''Actually they're more of a blue gray,'' Clay admitted, ''and I don't know why. There are a number of theories, but no one seems to know for sure. Alicia's parents are both dead, and she has no brothers or sisters, so the house was left in trust for Francie on her mother's death. I couldn't in all conscience sell it and move into something more manageable."

So Francie, as her mother's surviving heir, would receive a sizable inheritance when she reached twenty-one. Just one more chilling reason for Tamara not to tamper with the future she'd thrust upon her child at birth. Her daughter was a very wealthy little girl, and Tamara would never do anything to cast doubt, no matter how remote, on the child's right to inherit.

Later in the meal, Tamara broached the subject of Hertha's retirement. "I understand you're going to live with your daughter and her family in New Mexico."

Hertha nodded. "Yes, she has five children, one with Down's syndrome who requires special care, and she really needs my help. It's hard to leave here, though. I was with the Conrads before Alicia was born. She couldn't have been dearer to me if she'd been my own daughter, and Francie..." She reached out for the little girl's hand and squeezed it. "Francie is like one of my granddaughters." She shook her head as if to shake loose her sorrow. "But now my own family needs me, so I must go. Whoever takes my place had better treat Clay and my little girl right or I'll—"

Tamara smiled and interrupted. "I assure you that you won't have to worry about that if...if everything works out tonight. I love children." She noted that Clay sat quietly watching and listening, but saying nothing.

When dinner was finished, Clay turned Francie over to Hertha to be bathed and put to bed. "Come get me when you're ready and I'll tuck you in," he told the little girl, then escorted Tamara back across the entry hall into still another room.

This one was called the library for the obvious reason that the walls were lined with bookshelves filled with books. It was considerably smaller than the living room and featured a brick fireplace. Not as spectacular as the marble one, but it added to the cozier, more intimate feeling of this room, and Tamara felt much more relaxed and at home.

"Would you like a drink?" Clay asked, then let his gaze slide over her. "You are old enough, aren't you?"

She felt the familiar irritation that question always aroused. "Yes, Doctor, I'm old enough. I'm twenty-four, but people always assume that because I'm only five feet tall and weigh less than one hundred pounds I'm not grown-up yet."

He grinned. "Sorry. I can see it's a sore subject with you, but don't be in such a hurry to look older." His expression and tone changed to one of introspection. "It can happen quickly, and then you'll wish you looked young again."

She knew he was talking about himself. He must have aged considerably since his wife's death. Those white wings at his temples, which she found so attractive, were probably quite new. Such a shocking accident could do dreadful things to the survivors of the victim.

She sighed. "I suppose you're right, and now I'm going to reveal my total lack of sophistication by asking for a soda instead of a cocktail. I seldom drink anything stronger." She was afraid he'd think she was hopelessly immature, but instead he looked pleased.

"Don't apologize for that," he said sternly. "I admire you for going all the way through college without picking up any bad habits. I've noticed that you don't smoke, either."

Her mouth lifted at the corners in a half smile she couldn't completely suppress. She knew what he was trying to find out without actually asking it. Well, she'd save him the trouble. "No, and I've never done drugs. My parents had very staid, old-fashioned morals, and I was raised with strict values." She wondered if he'd be as impressed by her small-town naiveté if he ever found out that she'd had an illegitimate child when she was seventeen and then given it away. The thought was chilling.

"Will your parents approve of you spending the summer so far away from home?" Clay asked as he walked over to a small bar in the corner.

Tamara groaned inwardly. She should never have mentioned her parents. The last thing she wanted was to talk about her relationship with them, but she wasn't going to lie to him any more than she already had. "Clay, I make my own decisions. I haven't lived with Mom and Dad since I left home to go away to college six years ago. They are busy, productive people with full lives of their own." She regretted the combative edge her voice always took when she discussed her parents, and hoped he wouldn't pick up on it.

It was a vain hope. "I'm sorry," he said. "I'm still treating you like a teenager, aren't I? I didn't mean to. It's just that I'm an overprotective father myself, and I tend to think that's the way all parents are." He picked up two glasses and handed her one with something clear, sparkling and nonalcoholic in it. "Let's sit over here in front of the fire," he suggested.

The butter-soft leather sofa was placed so it faced the fireplace. It was like sinking into a cloud. She settled down with a long sigh and leaned her head against the back. Her gaze lifted and for the first time she saw the painting on the wall above the mantel.

It was a portrait of a slender young woman dressed in an ethereal-looking mauve gown and seated on a garden bench surrounded by green lawns and delicate flowering bushes in a riot of pastel colors. Her long golden hair fell over her shoulders all the way to the fullness of her breasts, and her lovely face was slightly turned so that her violet eyes seemed to be gazing dreamily into space.

Tamara caught her breath. "Oh, what a stunning portrait," she murmured, more to herself than to Clay.

"Yes, that's my wife, Alicia," he said softly as he sat down beside Tamara. "Her parents commissioned it the summer she graduated from college."

Tamara silently cursed herself for not thinking before she called attention to it. She should have suspected that it was his wife. It's no wonder he was so broken up over losing her. What man wouldn't be? Now all she could do was try to smooth it over and change to another subject as quickly as possible. "She was very beautiful" was all Tamara could think of to say before her mind went blank.

"Yes, she was. I suppose I should take the picture down and store it in the vault, but I don't want Francie to forget what her mother looked like." His tone was low, mournful.

Tamara felt a piercing jolt of jealousy. *No, I'm her mother! But you won't put up pictures of me so she won't forget me when I'm gone.*

She clamped her teeth together to keep from crying out her protest, and shame overcame the jealousy. She had no right to resent the woman who had taken as her own the child Tamara herself had given up. She should be grateful to Alicia Rutledge, and she was, but it was so hard to stand quietly by and hear another woman praised as her own daughter's mother.

Would she be making a big mistake if she stayed here and took care of Francie for the summer? Could she ever give her up again when fall came and it was time to go back to Iowa? Was she courting a grief even more intense than before?

A hand on her shoulder shook her slightly, startling her, and she jumped. "I don't think you've heard a word I've been saying," Clay chided as he removed his hand.

"Oh, I . . . I'm sorry," she apologized, embarrassed at being so rude. "I'm afraid I was thinking of something else. What were you saying to me?"

He looked somewhat perturbed. "I asked if you still want the job of temporary housekeeper you applied for."

"Of course I do. I want it very much," she was appalled to hear herself say.

Hold on there, you idiot. You've raised some pertinent questions about the advisability of staying here for the next two and a half months. Back off and give it more thought before you do something you may well regret.

"Then I have a few more questions for you," Clay said, "and I'm sure you must have some for me." He chuckled. "You haven't yet asked how much I'll pay you or what the job entails."

That's because she didn't care. She'd accept the position even if she had to pay him! So much for her nagging conscience.

She laughed, suddenly feeling free of the conflict that kept tormenting her. She'd take the job and worry about any consequences later. "Okay, so I'll ask. How much will you pay me, and what do I have to do for it?"

He laughed, too. "I hope you weren't this cavalier about salary and working conditions when you applied for your teaching position."

"I didn't have much choice about that," she told him. "As a beginning teacher, I had to take what the union bargained for. With you...well, I figure you'll provide me with food and shelter, and the shelter here is a lot more luxurious than what I provide for myself back home, so whatever salary I get will be pretty much frosting on the cake." He made a teasing face at her somewhat skewed reasoning, then told her what her wages would be. She was surprised. "I hate to tell you this, but you're more generous than I'd expected. I'll take it before you change your mind. Now, what am I supposed to do to earn all that money?"

"Ah, but don't forget," he cautioned her, "you'll be working a twenty-four-hour day seven days a week."

"Hey, that's not fair," she squealed in mock horror. "Haven't you heard of the Emancipation Proclamation?"

"Oh, damn," he muttered playfully. "Then I guess I'll have to give you weekends off, but your rations on those days will be cut to bread and water."

They both laughed then, and Tamara was delighted to see that Clay's expression had lost the shadow of sorrow and was as uninhibited as the sound of his laughter.

When they'd calmed down, Clay took a swallow of his whiskey, then returned the conversation to the highly informal interview. "Your duties will consist mainly of taking care of Francie during the week and fixing meals. I'll take over on weekends when you'll be free. I don't entertain guests. I haven't since Alicia died, and I don't plan to this summer. But, if something comes up and I need to entertain, I'll either take my guests out or have a meal catered."

Tamara wondered if he was trying to save her work, or if he thought she wasn't bright enough to plan and cook a formal dinner. He apparently didn't want his friends to get the idea that she was serving as his hostess.

"I have a cleaning crew come in every Thursday and clean the house," he continued, "so you won't have to do any of that, just keep the place looking reasonably neat. I'd appreciate it if you'd do the grocery shopping since you'll know what you want or need. I have an account at The Kaiser's Kitchen a few blocks from here, and I'll arrange for you to use it."

Tamara's eyes widened. "The Kaiser's Kitchen? Is that a restaurant or a market?"

He looked amused. "It's a market that serves the King William district where we're located. You probably don't know that the district was named after Kaiser Wilhelm, the ruler of Germany during the First World War and the grandson of Queen Victoria of England."

"How interesting," Tamara said. "And how tragic that the kaiser wound up fighting a war with the country his grandmother once ruled for so long."

As they each mulled over this fascinating piece of history, a childish voice from the hallway called, "Daddy, Daddy, I'm ready," and Francie, dressed in pajamas with

Disney's *Aladdin* splashed across the front, ran into the room and threw herself into her father's arms.

Clay hugged her and settled her on his lap. "Okay, kitten, I'll tuck you in and read you a story, but it will have to be a short one. We don't want to leave Tamara down here alone."

"She can come, too," the child announced, and Tamara's heart leapt with joy. She was going to help put her daughter to bed. That was something she'd dreamed of almost every night since giving her up.

"I'd love to," she said before Clay had a chance to say no.

The second story had closed doors on both sides of the hall. Lots of them. Tamara didn't know if they were all bedrooms, but surmised that most of them were. Clay stopped at the second one on the left and opened it. It was a room right out of a nursery rhyme, all pink and white, with gingham and ruffles and scaled-down furniture. Stuffed toys were everywhere, in every conceivable size and shape, and shelves on the walls displayed porcelain dolls elaborately dressed in exquisite hand-sewn outfits.

Tamara stifled a gasp as she entered the room. The Rutledges had given her child everything a little girl could ever want. She thought of her own three-room apartment in Ames. It was clean and neat and in a good neighborhood, but she could never have provided her daughter with so much luxury.

Francie Rutledge was living a fantasy. A fairy-tale life every mother dreamed of for her child but few could hope to afford. Obviously she'd made the right choice when she gave up her baby, so why didn't she feel vindicated?

On the other hand, would Francie ever learn to survive in the real world? Tamara immediately banished that thought. Thanks to Clay and his late wife, Alicia, Francie would never have to lower her standard of living.

Tamara sat on a child-size chair while Clay held Francie on his lap in an adult's rocker and read her a story. When he'd finished, he put the child in her canopied bed, tucked the covers around her and exchanged kisses.

After he'd said good-night and stood up, Francie held her arms out to Tamara. "I want to kiss you good-night, too," she said, and Tamara's knees gave way. Fortunately she was standing beside the bed at the time, so it looked as if she'd simply sat down. She gathered her daughter in her arms for the first time ever, and her eyes brimmed with tears that she had no hope of holding back as Francie clasped her around the neck and hugged.

The damp, childish kiss the youngster planted on Tamara's cheek was precious beyond compare, and she wondered if she'd ever be able to bring herself to wash her face again. She nuzzled the warm little neck and grazed the soft young lips with her own, then quickly wiped at her tears with the corner of the sheet before releasing the little girl.

She murmured good-night, then stood and hurried out of the room ahead of Clay. She needed a few seconds to pull herself together before he got a good look at her face. It would never do for him to see how emotional she was about his daughter. Too much could be as suspect as too little, and he was extremely particular about whom he hired to care for the child.

When he joined her in the hall he asked, "Would you like to see your room now?" At her nod, he then led her to the third door on the same side, opened it and flicked on the light. It was a charming room, not unlike the one she was staying in at the bed-and-breakfast inn. "The master bedroom is the first one at the top of the stairs on this side," he explained. "Then the nursery, and then this room. There weren't many bathrooms in these old houses, so you and Francie will share one that was added by knocking out two large closets between your rooms and remodeling. There's also another bathroom across the hall."

Tamara laughed. "In the house where I grew up in a small town in Iowa we had a single bathroom for the whole house.

Sharing with one small child won't be a problem at all. When do you want me to move in?"

"Let's go back downstairs and discuss it," he suggested.

Back in the library they again sat on the sofa and listened to the soft crackle of logs in the fire.

"Hertha is flying out of here on Sunday," he said after a few minutes, "but I'd like you to move in several days before that, if possible, so she can acquaint you with the house and the family idiosyncrasies and schedule."

Tamara cocked one eyebrow. "What do you mean by 'family idiosyncrasies'?"

He smiled. "Don't worry, there's nothing strange or bizarre. Just the little quirks that you find in any family, such as likes, dislikes, habits and tolerance levels. They'll be easier for you to learn if you work alongside Hertha for a couple of days or so."

"I guess I'll have to take your word for that," she teased, then became serious. "There's just one problem. If I'm going to spend all summer, I'll have to close up my apartment in Ames. I'll also need more clothes and a few other things."

Clay frowned. "Don't you have relatives or friends who could alert the apartment manager that you'll be gone, and then pack and send you the things you'll need?"

She thought a moment. "The only relatives I have are my father and mother, but they live halfway across the state from me. I do have friends who could do that, though. I'll call tomorrow and make arrangements."

"Great. Then feel free to move in anytime. Tomorrow, if you'd like."

Tamara was euphoric. She could move in here within a few hours and spend the rest of the summer with Francie and Clay!

Whoa there, Tamara, back up. You're not coming here to flirt with Clayton Rutledge. He has nothing to do with your reasons for staying here. Your daughter is your only concern, and don't you forget it. She knew that her prickly conscience was right, even though she did resent being chastised by it.

"Thank you," she said somewhat meekly, as if he'd been able to read her thoughts. "Let me see about having things taken care of back home, and I'll get in touch with you sometime tomorrow. Is it all right if I call you at the office?"

"Fine," Clay agreed. "I'll alert Hertha that you might be moving in tomorrow."

Tamara looked around. "By the way, where is Hertha?"

"I imagine she has the kitchen cleaned up by now and is upstairs in her room," he said. "Hers is the one across the hall from Francie's. She spends most of her evenings up there. I think she enjoys the privacy. It's large and she has it fixed up like a studio apartment."

Tamara looked at her watch and was surprised to see that it was almost ten o'clock. "Oh my," she said, "it's getting late, and I'd hoped to still make some phone calls tonight. I'd better get back to the inn."

She stood, and Clay rose with her. "Will you be able to find your way back in the dark?" he asked.

She couldn't tell him that she had the route between his home and the inn memorized from driving so often past his house hoping for a glimpse of Francie. "Oh, yes," she assured him instead as they walked into the entry hall. "I'm good at keeping directions straight." When they reached the door, he opened it and she stepped outside, then turned back to face him. Hesitantly she put out her hand, unsure of how to deal with him now that he was her employer. "Thank you, Dr. Rutledge, for giving me this summer job. You won't be sorry, I promise."

He took her hand, but instead of shaking it and letting go he held it. "My name's Clay, remember? And I'm the one who's thanking you for helping me out of a serious bind. I would have had to send Francie to the ranch to stay with my parents if you hadn't come along, and I don't think I could have stood being separated from her for such a long time."

He sounded so sad and lonely that she could hardly resist the temptation to take that one small step that would touch her body against his, and then put her arms around him. She was almost sure he'd respond. She could feel it in the tension that radiated between them. But when the embrace was over, he'd rescind his agreement and send her back to Iowa. That was the thought she couldn't stand.

Slowly, regretfully, she slid her hand from his, murmured good-night and almost ran to her car.

Chapter Four

Clay stood at the open door watching until Tamara's car was out of sight, then closed it and expelled a long, painful sigh. What in hell had gotten into him taking such a beautiful young woman, and a stranger at that, into his home?

It was true he was desperate for a housekeeper-cum-baby-sitter, but he couldn't shake the feeling that he'd made a mistake in inviting this particular woman into his life. For one thing, he hadn't realized how attractive, or how young she was the other day in his office when she was swathed in that ugly plastic bib and had her mouth held open by dental instruments. Tonight he'd been startled by her beauty. Small and exquisite, she was like a fragile porcelain doll.

She'd only had to look at him with those huge, lustrous, deep brown eyes, and he'd caved in and hired her without considering the consequences. And consequences there were bound to be. She didn't look strong enough or old enough to give full-time care to his house and child. Francie was a healthy, boisterous youngster who took a lot of running after.

On the other hand, Tamara was a schoolteacher experienced at handling children Francie's age. But even if she was perfectly capable of managing the job he'd assigned her, there was another more pressing problem. Ms. Houston was not only too immature and too beautiful, but both he and she were too young to live in the same house together with only a child to chaperon!

That thought made him squirm. It had been niggling at him all evening, but he'd resolutely pushed it aside until now. He didn't like what it implied. When Alicia died, his sexual desire had died with her, and he liked it that way. He could never love another woman the way he'd loved his wife. She'd been the center of his being, his dearest friend, his only sweetheart and his beloved life partner.

Until tonight, even the thought of making love with any woman other than Alicia had repulsed him, but this young lady had shown him that he wasn't immune to the basic biological urges after all. He'd been appalled when he'd recognized the stirring of his body after a year of abstinence, and he'd immediately put some distance between them and changed the direction of his thoughts.

Then he'd gone right ahead and hired her anyway.

Good God, how stupid could a man be? He'd probably better call her in the morning and tell her he'd changed his mind. She'd be upset and he wouldn't blame her, but in the long run it would be for the best.

Late the following morning, Clay was called to the phone at his office. He seldom took calls while working on a patient, but the receptionist said it was Tamara Houston and he felt too guilty not to talk to her.

He'd lain awake most of the night before thinking of ways to tell her why he wasn't going to hire her after all, but they all sounded cruel and contrived. When he wakened that morning, he'd intended to get in touch with her early before she made arrangements to move but somehow he hadn't found the time to do it.

No, that wasn't true. He could have made the time, but he hadn't. He'd used every excuse he could think of to delay, and now it was too late to get out of the arrangement with any shred of dignity.

He went into his office and picked up the phone. "Tamara, I've been meaning to call you—"

"Oh, that's all right," she interrupted, apparently misinterpreting his comment. "You probably wouldn't have been able to get through anyway. I've been on the phone to Iowa all morning, but I've finally arranged with a friend to close up my apartment and pack and ship my summer clothes along with some personal items...."

He was struck by her voice. She even sounded like a little girl, breathless and excited, as if she was embarking on a great adventure.

"I'm just calling to let you know that I'll be checking out of here in a few minutes," she continued nonstop, without giving him a chance to get a word in edgewise, "and then, if it's all right with you and Hertha, I'll take my things over to your house. You did tell Hertha I was coming, didn't you?"

"No, I... That is, I..." Oh, what the hell. He couldn't back out of the deal now. He didn't want to disappoint her, although for the life of him he couldn't figure out why she was so excited about working as his housekeeper and baby-sitter.

"I'll call her right now and let her know you're coming," he promised, and for some reason he felt as if a great load had been lifted from him. "Welcome to the family, Tamara."

For the rest of the week Tamara worked alongside Hertha, learning the layout of the house, Clay and Francie's likes and dislikes in food and other things, and the proper

rotocol for the household help. Hertha was insistent on the
atter.

"Don't ever forget your place," she advised. "Clayton is
friendly and informal employer, but you're not a member
f the family. Not wife, relative or even friend. You're an
mployee, and that's all you'll ever be no matter how well
e treats you. You'll avoid a lot of heartache by remember-
g that."

Tamara knew the advice was good, but unfortunately she
as already too mired in the relationships of this family to
eed it. Not only was she the birth mother of the child, but
he was becoming more attracted to that child's adoptive
ather every day. It would trigger a real blowup if Clay ever
ound out.

Hertha left for New Mexico on Sunday as scheduled, and
or the next week everything was fine during the day when
amara's sweetest dream came true and she could spend
ninterrupted hours with her little daughter. But the eve-
ings were awkward.

The routine seldom varied. Clay usually arrived home
etween five and six and spent time with Francie while Ta-
1ara cooked dinner. After they'd eaten, Francie either
layed outside with the next-door neighbor's children or
vatched television in the family room off the kitchen. Clay
usied himself working in the yard or at his desk in the li-
rary, while Tamara cleared the table and did the dishes.

At eight she gave Francie her bath then turned her over to
er father, who read to her and tucked her into bed. It was
fter that that the awkwardness set in.

From then until he went to bed, Clay spent the time in the
brary reading, watching television or sometimes talking on
he phone. Tamara wasn't sure if she should join him or if
e preferred that she stay in her room. It was a large room
vith two lounge chairs and a television as well as a double
ed, chest of drawers and vanity. It was comfortable, and

she could hear Francie if she should be restless or cry out but it was also lonely.

Tamara was gregarious by nature. She liked to be with other people. She enjoyed visiting and exchanging views, gossip, recipes, but even more, she wanted to be with Clay. He was lonely, too. He must be. How could he not, sitting downstairs all alone in this big old house? Surely he'd welcome company. He'd never told her he wanted to be left alone, but neither had he asked her to join him.

That weekend was her first time off, and Clay wouldn't even let her fix breakfast. "You worked right through last weekend what with Hertha leaving and everything so chaotic," he reminded her as they stood in the kitchen where he'd caught her making coffee. "But now you're free to do anything you please."

"It pleases me to cook breakfast for you and Francie," she told him as he took the coffeepot from her and finished adding the ground beans.

He stopped and looked at her. "That's very sweet of you," he said solemnly, "but you need your time off. Get out and see the city, go to a movie, take a boat ride on the river—"

"Clay, I can do all of that and still get breakfast," she interrupted. "Besides, I don't have anybody to do things with. It's not much fun to wander around all by myself."

"Mmm," he muttered thoughtfully. "So it's company you want. How about if Francie and I take you on a tour of the town? Or are you sick to death of us by now?"

"Don't be silly," she exclaimed. "I'd love that, but I didn't mean . . . That is, you don't have to—"

"I know I don't have to," he agreed, "but I'd like to. I used to enjoy showing the city to out-of-towners, but it's been a long time. . . ." His voice trailed off, and she knew he hadn't been getting out much since his wife died. It would do him good to start mingling again.

"Clay, I'd be delighted to go sightseeing with you and Francie if you're sure...that is..."

The shadow of a smile hovered around the corners of his mouth as he put his hand under her chin and lifted her face to his. "Tamara, I'm sure. I'd like to spend the day with you."

Their gazes met and clung, and the warmth in his eyes dissolved her resolution to keep her distance and be a proper employee. The attraction between them was too strong. She felt her chin quiver in his hand, but she was powerless to look away.

He wanted to kiss her. She couldn't be wrong about that. The pull was not only powerful but mutual. She might not be very experienced in these things, but neither had she been living in a nunnery. She'd been kissed enough times to know when a man was hungry for her caress, but this was the first time she'd wanted it with the same urgent hunger.

Her eyes closed and her lips parted as she envisioned his mouth covering hers, but the groan that seemed torn from him was one of frustration instead of pleasure. Her eyes flew open as he turned away from her. "I'll wake up Francie," he said, his voice raw, and walked quickly out of the room.

By the time he came back with Francie, dressed and bubbling with excitement over the prospect of spending the day sightseeing with her dad and Tamara, she had the bacon broiled, the eggs scrambled and the oatmeal thick and hot.

An hour later, after they were well fed and the kitchen was clean again, the three of them piled into Clay's black Cadillac. "The closest place to start is the Alamo," he told Tamara. "It's only a few blocks away, right in the middle of town. Have you seen it yet?"

"I've driven by it, but I haven't been inside," she said.

"My class at school went there on a field trip," Francie chimed in from the back seat where she was firmly fastened down by a seat belt. "My teacher said it's also called The

Cradle of Texas...uh...of Texas...*Liberty*," she exclaimed triumphantly.

Tamara's pride in her bright little daughter knew no bounds. "That's right, it is," she confirmed. "The Texans fought Mexico for their liberty twice. They were badly outnumbered and lost the siege of the Alamo, but a little more than a month later they won the battle at San Jacinto and Texas later became a territory of the United States of America."

Clay glanced at her with amusement as he started the motor. "For a Yankee, you're pretty well versed in Texas history. A lot of our young tourists have never heard of the Alamo before."

"I'm a teacher," she reminded him. "Besides, with Houston as my last name, it's no wonder I'm interested in this state."

Clay chuckled and backed the car out of the garage. "Are you also aware that the Alamo was not only a fort but also a Spanish mission? The first one in San Antonio. It's more properly known as Mission San Antonio de Valero."

"My teacher said a mission is a church," Francie informed them, "but people lived there, too."

When they reached their destination, Clay parked near Alamo Plaza, the cobblestone area in front of the restored structure, and they went inside. It was smaller than Tamara had imagined, with cell-size rooms opening off the main one. Hard to believe that nearly two hundred volunteers could have been packed into the space. The fact that those dedicated patriots were actually able to hold off a Mexican army of thousands for thirteen days before the Texans were all killed was mind-blowing. No wonder the battle cry of the Texans from then on was "Remember the Alamo!"

After they left the Alamo, they walked the short distance to Paseo del Rio, the Riverwalk. "The San Antonio River used to be something of an eyesore running through the middle of town," Clay explained as he led Tamara and

Francie down a flight of concrete steps to a veritable garden one level below the busy city streets. "Now it's our most popular tourist attraction."

"I can see why," Tamara said as she viewed the charming walkways winding along the natural curves of the river on both sides, and fronting a myriad of luxury hotels, boutiques, galleries and restaurants. They took a cruise on one of the flat-bottom open riverboats that meandered through midtown. They passed beneath the giant cyprus trees and palms, taking in the lovely foliage that surrounded the shore. Tamara was enchanted. She'd never seen anything like this in Iowa. "Oh, Clay, it's so beautiful. Imagine a tropical paradise in the heart of one of the biggest cities in the country!"

"Yes," he agreed. "It was a stroke of genius on the part of the city fathers to make use of the river's potential—" He broke off what he was saying and pointed ahead of them. "Watch up there as we go by. That open-air patio-type stage on the right bank of the river is the Arneson River Theatre, and the tiers of grass seats on the other side is where the audience sits. Listen, you can hear the music. A group of Mexican folk dancers must be performing."

As they drew closer, Tamara could hear the music and see the colorfully costumed dancers on the stage, and sure enough, sitting directly across the river was the audience, clapping along with the music and enjoying themselves. "How unique," she exclaimed. "I've never heard of anything like it."

"I don't believe there is another theater quite like it," Clay said.

They had a leisurely lunch at the revolving restaurant on top of the Tower of the Americas in HemisFair Plaza where the view was almost limitless. Then they spent the rest of the afternoon at Brackenridge Park where Francie played on the vintage carousel as well as other rides in the kiddie park section. When she tired of that they all rode the skyride to the adjoining zoo.

By the time they arrived home late that afternoon, they were hot, grimy and tired. "You two young ladies are going to make an old man of me at this rate," Clay groused as he pulled into the garage, shut off the motor and unfastened his seat belt. "I'd forgotten what hard work sightseeing can be."

"Sorry about that," Tamara said with a grin that was anything but repentant. "Will you need help limping into the house? If Francie gets on one side of you and I get on the other, I think we can drag you in—"

"Oh, you do, do you?" he growled, but she saw the wicked gleam in his eye and ducked just as he lunged across the seat for her. "I'll show you who's decrepit...." He caught her and leaned over her. She screamed with laughter and squirmed to get away from him as he blew on the side of her neck, sending tickles down her spine.

"Daddy, Daddy, you're hurting her." It was Francie, and there was genuine fear in her tone. "Please, don't hurt Tamara!"

Both Clay and Tamara bolted upright, shocked by the child's mistaken distress. "He's not hurting me," Tamara hastened to assure Francie as she unfastened her own seat belt and twisted around to look at the little girl in the back. Francie had released her seat belt and was standing up. "Oh, honey, we were just playing," Tamara tried explaining as she got to her knees and hugged her. "We were teasing each other. Your daddy would never hurt me."

"Of course I wouldn't," Clay said as he stroked the child's head. "We were just pretending to wrestle."

Francie's lower lip still quivered. "But she was crying."

"No, sweetheart, I wasn't crying," Tamara quickly informed her. "I was laughing. See, no tears." She widened her eyes and pointed to them.

"Well...okay." Francie apparently wasn't totally convinced yet as she turned to look at her father. "Then you'd better kiss and make up."

Tamara couldn't tell if it was she or Clay who was the most startled. She saw the shock and embarrassment in his expression, and was sure it mirrored her own. She just prayed that the momentary flash of hopeful excitement she'd felt hadn't shown.

"Honey, I—"

"That's not necessary—"

They both spoke at once, then Clay stopped while she continued. "We don't need to make up because we were only pretending to fight."

Clay nodded in agreement, but Francie wasn't persuaded. "Yes, you do. If you were pretending to fight, then you have to pretend to kiss and make up."

It was obvious that she wasn't going to take no for an answer. Tamara and Clay looked at each other. He was pink with embarrassment, and she knew she was, too. "The kid's got a point," he said in a somewhat strangled tone. "Do you mind?"

She couldn't seem to catch her breath enough to answer, but of its own accord her body leaned into his. Their glances caught, and her lips parted as he raised his hand and stroked her cheek. Then his arm pulled her closer as he lowered his head and brushed her mouth with his.

It was a feathery touch that would have satisfied Francie's requirement, but it did much more to Tamara's senses. The kiss was sweet but not innocent. His touch did amazing things to her nervous system. Feelings she'd never experienced before flooded through her, and she responded instantly, but the kiss only lasted a few seconds.

"Now are you satisfied, young lady?" he asked Francie as he pulled away from Tamara.

"I guess so," she answered, "but you didn't say 'I'm sorry.'"

He rubbed his cheek in Tamara's hair. "But I'm not sorry," he said, aiming for a light tone although his voice still shook. "It was a very nice kiss."

Francie laughed with childish delight. "Oh, Daddy, I mean you didn't say you were sorry for hurting her."

"I didn't hurt her," he repeated firmly. "She told you that and so did I."

"Then why did you kiss her?"

Tamara stifled a giggle as Clay sighed in exasperation. "Because she's a very kissable lady and I couldn't resist, okay?" he blurted.

He squeezed Tamara quickly then released her. "Now get a move on, both of you, and get in the house. We can't sit here in the garage playing games the rest of the day."

Tamara laughed and scrambled out of the car, but she was a little hurt, too. Of course that episode had started out as a game, but the minute Francie insisted that she and Clay kiss it had stopped being a charade for her. It had for him, too. She could tell by his reaction when their mouths met and clung, but he obviously wasn't going to admit it.

Clay didn't allude to the incident again until they'd tucked Francie into bed later that evening. After Tamara had bathed the child and savored the elation of sharing goodnight hugs and kisses with her little daughter, she started to leave the room as Clay settled down on the side of the bed to read Francie a story.

Tamara was halfway to the door when he called to her. "Tamara, I'd like to speak to you in the library when I'm finished here." His words were polite, but she heard the strain in his tone.

"Yes, of course," she answered as she walked away. Now what? she wondered as she descended the stairs. Was he going to make an issue of that kiss after all? Surely he wouldn't be angry with her. Or would he?

One of the things she'd learned from her traumatic experience with rape was that she couldn't rely on her judgment of men. She'd actually had a crush on her attacker and had no idea he was capable of such a degrading assault. Not that she was afraid of Clay, but she could be very wrong in thinking he'd been as affected by their kiss as she had.

She was sitting on the sofa trying to concentrate on reading the newspaper when Clay joined her in the library. He went straight to the bar and started assembling ingredients for a drink. "What do you like in your Shirley Temple?" he asked.

She chuckled. "Why don't you surprise me."

He grinned. "Okay, but you're taking a big chance. Shirley Temples aren't exactly my specialty."

Tamara was relieved at his impish tone. Apparently he wasn't angry or upset. Maybe he just wanted company after all. That impression didn't last long after he handed her a tall glass of mixed fruit juices topped with whipped cream and a maraschino cherry, then sat down beside her.

He took a swallow of his own drink, then twisted it nervously between his hands and looked straight ahead as he spoke. "Tamara...I...I told Francie I wasn't going to apologize for kissing you, but on second thought, I may be taking too much for granted. What I'm trying to say is...just because it was a warm and pleasing experience for me doesn't mean it was for you, too." She gasped with surprise and tried to interrupt, but he hurried on. "No, hear me out. If I offended you in any way, then I most certainly do ask your forgiveness."

Tamara was amazed. He really was afraid that he might have offended her. How could he possibly think that? She'd been as enthusiastic a participant as he. Instinctively she reached out and put her hand on his arm. "Clay, you seem to be forgetting something. I wasn't exactly fighting you off." She tried for a teasing tone but wasn't very successful.

He looked at her then, and she saw the uncertainty in his brown eyes. "I haven't forgotten," he said quietly. "It was your sweet and caring response that shattered my control, but that doesn't mean you wanted me to...to come on to you," he finished in a rush.

Her fingers caressed his arm. "You weren't coming on to me. At least, that wasn't the impression I got."

His gaze sought and held hers. "I hope I wasn't. I never intended to, but once I had you in my arms, your mouth trembling beneath mine..."

His words trailed off as the magnetism between them seemed to draw them together once more.

Clay muttered an oath and pulled his arm away from her touch. He raked his fingers through his hair. "There's something you need to know, Tamara. I was very much in love with my wife. We'd been married for almost fourteen years, and the marriage was a happy one. When she was killed so suddenly, it nearly destroyed me. If it hadn't been for Francie, I don't think I could have gone on."

He set his glass on the coffee table and stood. "Alicia and I grew up together," he continued as he started to pace, "although she lived here in town and my parents are ranchers. Her maternal grandparents owned the ranch next to ours, and she spent summers and holidays with them. Once we were old enough to drive cars, we saw even more of each other, and we attended the university at Austin together."

He paused and stood quietly looking up at his wife's portrait. Tamara was beginning to think he'd forgotten she was in the room with him until he spoke again. This time his tone was low as if he was musing aloud.

"Neither of us ever had a serious relationship with anyone else. We always took it for granted that when we grew up we'd get married, and that's what we did. The wedding took place less than a month after we graduated, and we moved to Los Angeles where we earned our advanced degrees."

Tamara listened, eager to learn as much about him as possible, but the two questions she couldn't ask, he didn't broach. *Why did they adopt a baby instead of having one of their own? And, if one of them was infertile, which one was it?*

Clay stopped pacing and stood with his hands in his pockets, staring into the unlit fireplace. His shoulders were slightly hunched, and he looked so... so alone.

She put her drink beside his and walked over to stand beside him. "Clay, I'm so sorry...." The sound of her voice startled him. He jumped, and she realized that he truly *had* forgotten she was there.

"I'm not asking for sympathy," he said somewhat grimly. "I have a point to make, but I'm afraid I've been rambling."

She couldn't let him think he'd been boring her. "Oh, no—"

"What I'm trying to tell you," he interrupted, "is that I miss Alicia and the—" again he faltered and his face reddened "—the intimate relationship we had." It was obviously difficult for him to talk about such a personal and private subject. "We were extremely close. We were nearly always together when we weren't working, and we were very... um... tactile," he finished lamely. "We did a lot of hugging and kissing and just plain touching.... Oh, damn!" He growled in frustration as he started to pace again. "I don't know how to put this."

He turned and glared at her, but she understood that it was in frustration rather than in anger. "It's been over a year since I've enjoyed a woman's loving caress." He spoke rapidly as if he needed to say it and get it over with. "I don't mean sex, although there's that, too, but I feel just as deprived of the nonerotic touching. When Francie urged me to kiss you, I thought I could handle it, but you were so soft, so cuddly and warm...." His glance softened and he sighed. "If it means anything to you, I'm not sure I could have let you go when I did, if we hadn't been so well chaperoned.

"What I'm trying to tell you, Tamara, is that you sti
feelings in me I thought were dead. I suppose I should b
grateful for that, but I'm not. It just complicates every
thing. I have no intention of marrying again. I could neve
love another woman the way I did Alicia, but neither woul
I settle for anything less. An intimate live-in relationship i
out of the question. That's not the example I want to set fo
my daughter."

Tamara was delighted to hear that he had strong feeling
for her, but he was telling her in no uncertain terms tha
those feelings were unacceptable to him. Did that mean h
was going to fire her and send Francie to the ranch until h
could find permanent help? Oh, God, she hoped not
Should she ask him or just keep quiet and hope the though
hadn't crossed his mind?

No, she couldn't do that. The suspense of not knowing i
he might decide to send her away would drive her crazy
"Clay," she began, "are you going to change your min
about letting me work here this summer?"

She held her breath as he hesitated, but then he shook hi
head. "No." His tone was regretful but firm. "Believe me
I've thought about it. I even came to the conclusion that
should, but you're so good with Francie and she already
seems devoted to you. Also, I haven't found anyone else I'
trust to care for her, so I guess I'm—" He snapped hi
mouth shut before he could finish the sentence.

"Stuck with me?" she said acidly, and knew she'
guessed right when she saw the chagrin in his expressiv
face.

"Damn, Tamara," he exploded. "Don't make this an
harder than it already is. If you want to quit, I won't try t
stop you, but if you decide to stay, I guarantee that there wil
be no replay of what happened this afternoon." Cla
stomped out of the room and out of the house. The doo
slammed behind him as he practically flew down the steps
and headed for the gate.

What in hell had gotten into him? He'd started to explain his feelings for Alicia and the grief he still felt over her death as a means of softening the blow for Tamara when he dismissed her. He left the yard and stalked down the sidewalk. He'd even admitted his tender feelings toward *her* because he didn't want her to think she was in any way to blame for that dismissal, but the more he talked the harder it was for him to get to the point. Instead of simply saying, "Sorry, Tamara, but this isn't working out," and giving her a hefty severance check, he'd hemmed and hawed and skirted the subject until he heard himself practically pleading with her to stay.

Maybe the loneliness was finally getting to him. This past year had been hell, but that was no reason for him to seek solace with a girl like Tamara. Well, she wasn't actually a girl, but compared to him she was. Twenty-four seemed awfully young when you were thirty-seven. And what's more, she was an employee living in his home. He'd be a real bastard if he seduced her—

Seduced her! Where did that thought come from? The idea had never even crossed his mind.

Chapter Five

Quitting was never an option for Tamara, but during th
next week she sometimes wished it was. The awkwardnes
that had bothered her the first week of her employment i
the Rutledge home was now downright oppressive. The un
dercurrent of embarrassment over their situation ha
erected a wall between Clay and Tamara that made ther
virtual strangers living in the same house.

Clay's formerly friendly manner had become stiff an
cool but so had hers. He was obviously avoiding her. He n
longer ate breakfast with her and Francie, and twice tha
week he hadn't come home for dinner. When that hap
pened, he was thoughtful enough to call and let her know h
wouldn't be there, but he never said where he was going. Sh
was dismayed at how much the stab of jealousy hurt at th
thought that he might be dating someone. On the nights h
was home, the conversation was stilted and mostly aimed a
Francie. After the child was in bed, he retreated even mor
pointedly into the library and made no effort to include her

By Friday evening Tamara was feeling both ignored and lonely. If it hadn't been for Francie, she would have given her notice and gone back to Iowa, but there was nothing she wouldn't endure to prolong this reunion with her daughter for as long as she possibly could.

Unfortunately her feelings for her employer kept escalating in spite of his polite withdrawal from her. She understood that he wasn't deliberately being rude. He was just protecting himself from becoming involved with a woman, no matter how temporarily, and running the risk of caring too much again.

But his vulnerability only made him all the more attractive.

That evening the phone rang while they were still eating, and Clay answered it in the kitchen. She heard him say, "Hello," then, "Oh, hi, Mom, what's up?"

"It's Grandma," Francie exclaimed excitedly as she jumped out of her chair and headed for the kitchen. "Hey, Daddy, let me talk to her, too."

Tamara felt like an eavesdropper sitting in the dining room listening to the one-sided conversation, and she tried to shut it out and think of something else. Then, after Francie had talked for a few minutes, she heard Clay say, "But, Mom, that's her day off. She probably has other plans," and realized he was talking about her.

Tamara had never met Clay's parents. Their ranch was about fifty miles from San Antonio so they didn't see each other all that often, but she'd noticed that they talked on the phone every few days. Clay had mentioned that he had two brothers who also lived and worked on the ranch, but when she'd asked him why he'd chosen an unrelated profession over the family business, he just shrugged and muttered something about not being a born rancher like the rest of them.

Now that she knew they were talking about her, her interest zeroed in and refused to be sidetracked. He was silent for a moment, then spoke again. "Look, Mom, I don't like to intrude on her days off, but Francie and I would love to come. We could even spend the whole weekend."

Resentment flared in Tamara. He wasn't even going to ask her if she'd care to do whatever it was his mother was proposing. She didn't like having someone else make her decisions.

His mother must have had quite a bit to say on the subject because he didn't speak for several moments, and when he did, he sounded disgruntled. "Oh, for... That's not the case at all. If anything she's overqualified. She's a teacher for God's sake—"

Tamara's eyes widened. Clay's mother apparently thought he wasn't capable of choosing the right person to look after her little granddaughter. *Her little granddaughter.* But Francie wasn't Clay's mother's granddaughter. She was Tamara's mother's granddaughter.

The familiar bitterness washed over her, and she bit her lip to keep from crying out. No. Margaret Houston had given up any claim to her only grandchild long before Francie was born. She hadn't wanted the "disgrace" of an out-of-wedlock baby in the family. The regard of her narrow-minded friends and neighbors had been more important to her than her own granddaughter.

"Tamara!" She jumped as a hand caught her shoulder and Clay's raised voice broke through her troubling thoughts. She looked up, surprised to see him standing over her. "I'm sorry," he apologized and removed his hand. " didn't mean to startle you, but you looked so... Are you all right?"

"Oh, yes, of course," she said breathlessly. "I'm sorry my mind was wandering...." She could hear Francie talking to her grandmother on the phone again, and hastened to ask, "Did you want something?"

"That's my mother calling. She's been wanting to meet you ever since you came to us, and she's invited you, Fran

:ie and me to a barbecue at the ranch on Sunday. I told her
t was your day off, but—''

"I haven't made any plans. I'd love to go," Tamara in-
:errupted, delighted at the chance to meet Clay's family,
Francie's extended family. The grandparents, uncles, aunts
and possibly cousins she'd never have had if Tamara had
been allowed to raise her.

Clay looked somewhat unsettled. "Oh. Good. Well then,
I'll tell her we'll all be there."

Tamara awakened early Sunday morning to thunder,
lightning and thick dark clouds that looked as if they were
going to release torrents of rain any minute.

Oh, no. Did this mean they wouldn't go to the ranch after all? A barbecue implied outdoor cooking and eating, but
surely it could be moved inside if the weather was bad. It
had only rained a couple of times since she'd been in San
Antonio. Clay had commented on the dryness and said it
was unusual since June was one of their wettest months. But
why did it have to cloud up and pour today of all days?

She was going to be sorely disappointed if their outing was
canceled. She'd been eagerly looking forward to seeing the
ranch where Clay had grown up, and getting to know the
people who would help shape Francie's life during her
growing-up years. That thought depressed Tamara since she
would have no input at all in the raising of her daughter after this summer.

She was also aware that she was abusing Clay's good nature by agreeing so readily to this outing when she knew he
didn't want her along. After all, she was only the housekeeper. He had no obligation to include her in his family or
social plans.

The clouds opened up and rain pelted down as she dressed
in the jeans and plaid shirt Clay had suggested last night
when she'd asked him what she should wear. She was just

going to assume that the storm wouldn't stop them and hope she was right.

Tamara had breakfast ready by the time Clay and Fran-cie came downstairs. Both were dressed in jeans, western-style shirts, boots and cowboy hats. She breathed a sigh of relief. Apparently Texans were too hardy a breed to let a little bad weather change their plans.

Clay eyed her with an appreciative gleam. "You look great," he commented slowly as his gaze roamed over her diminutive form. "I don't suppose you have any boots?"

She grinned. "I don't have much call for boots in Ames."

He chuckled. "No, I guess you don't. Those tennis shoes will be okay. They look sturdy. But you'll need a hat. No self-respecting Texan would ride the range without the obligatory Stetson."

"What do you mean, 'ride the range'?" Tamara yipped, only half-teasing. "It's raining. Besides, I'm a town girl. I've never been on a horse."

This time Clay let loose with a full-blown laugh. "Then you've got a treat coming. We'll make a cowgirl of you yet. As for the storm, we have plenty of rain gear at the ranch."

"Daddy, I'll bet one of Mommy's hats would fit Ta-mara," Francie said eagerly. Both Clay and Tamara were shocked into silence.

Clay blanched and shook his head, but when he spoke, his voice was calm though a little shaky. "We gave your moth-er's clothes to the Red Cross, remember?"

"Oh, yeah." Francie sounded disappointed but not es-pecially sad. She obviously found it easier to talk about the loss of her mother than her father did.

They left for the ranch shortly after they'd finished eat-ing and Clay had stacked the dirty dishes in the dishwasher. He was still adamant about Tamara not working on her days off.

Halfway to their destination, the rain stopped and the clouds started growing lighter. By the time they turned off the two-lane paved county highway onto a private dirt road, it was obvious that no moisture had fallen here at all. Eventually the road led to a gate with a sign above that read Rocking R Ranch and was illustrated with a capital *R* with a rocker underneath.

A big, white, two-story house nestled in a grove of huge old trees came into view. Tamara figured the trees must have been planted many years ago to shade the house and surrounding buildings since the rest of the area was barren prairie for as far as she could see.

Clay parked the car beside the detached garage, but before he could even turn off the engine, Francie had unfastened her seat belt and scrambled out the door. "Grandma, Grandma," she called to the tall, slender woman in jeans and red-and-white-checked shirt who had appeared on the wraparound porch, "we brought Tamara."

"Grandma" hunkered down and hugged the child while Clay and Tamara walked more sedately to the house and up the porch steps. Mrs. Rutledge stood and embraced Clay, then turned to Tamara. Her blue eyes widened, and a look of surprise flitted across her angular face as she put out her hand. "I'm Ruth Rutledge," she said without waiting for Clay to introduce them, "and you must be Tamara?"

Tamara took her hand. It was a ranch woman's hand, brown and callused, with a strong, firm grip. "Tamara Houston," she confirmed. "I'm very pleased to meet you, Mrs. Rutledge."

"Ruth," she said absently. "We're all one big family around here, but I thought you were...that is, Clay told me you're a teacher, but that can't be. You're not old enough."

Ruth Rutledge was an attractive woman who was probably in her sixties since Clay had told Tamara that he had an older as well as a younger brother, but she didn't look her age. There were sprinklings of white in her dark hair, but it was cropped short in a modified pixie cut that highlighted her prominent cheekbones and determined chin. Surprisingly the only lines in her smooth tan face were the fine lines at the corners of her snapping eyes.

"I'm twenty-four and teach second grade in Ames, Iowa," Tamara said almost without thinking since she'd repeated it so many times. "I look younger because I'm small. When I was ten, people thought I was seven, and now I'm still taken for a teenager."

She'd apparently sounded more annoyed than she'd intended because Clay's formidable mother suddenly looked uncomfortable. "I'm sorry," she apologized. "I can see how that would get to be frustrating, but looking younger does have its compensations. Wait until you're my age. You'll be happy about it then." She turned and opened the screen door. "Come on inside," she said as she reached for Francie's hand and led the way. "The coffee's on and Juanita's baked your favorite cinnamon rolls, Clay. They're just hot out of the oven."

As Tamara and Clay walked along behind her, Tamara observed that Ruth was almost as tall as her son. Her slender waist curved in, unlike most women her age who had borne children.

"Mmm," Clay moaned rapturously as they stepped into the entryway and were assailed with the sweet, cinnamony aroma of the freshly baked pastry. "I've missed Juanita's cinnamon rolls." He looked around the room, then asked, "Where's Dad?"

"He and Jim are out mending fences," Ruth answered. "They should be back any time now."

In the roomy, old-fashioned kitchen, Clay and Francie embraced the middle-aged woman whom they introduced as Juanita, the cook and housekeeper. She was matronly built with black hair, which she wore parted in the middle and fashioned into a bun at the back of her neck.

"Sit down and eat the rolls I baked just for you," she insisted and gestured toward the heavy walnut table with its matching chairs.

The pastry was warm and delicious, and the conversation around the table was lively but of little interest to Tamara, who soon gave up trying to sort out the people and the events they talked about. During a lull, she leaned over and asked Francie if she'd like to show her around the barnyard that she'd noticed when they drove up.

"Yeah," the child exclaimed, "that'd be fun. They have horses, an' cows, an' pigs, an' chickens, an'—"

"Whoa, there," Tamara said with a laugh. "I'm sure they have, so let's go see them."

"Okay," Francie agreed as she wiggled out of her chair. She walked over to her father and pulled on his sleeve to get his attention. "Daddy, Tamara and me are going outside. I'm gonna show her the horses, an' the cows, an'..."

She continued the litany as Clay looked up, startled, when Tamara slid her chair back. He glanced from her to his daughter. "But I was going to show her around," he told Francie.

"That's okay," she said magnanimously, "you can come, too."

Clay wrinkled his nose at her. "Thanks a bunch," he muttered as he stood up. "You want to come, Ma."

Ruth shook her head. "No, thanks. I'll help Juanita get dinner started."

Francie led them out the kitchen door and across the yard to the enormous red barn. Clay walked with his hand at the back of Tamara's waist, which surprised her since he hadn't touched her since that heart-stopping kiss. She was careful not to call his attention to the contact even though it sent shivers up and down her spine. He'd almost certainly remove his hand if she did, and she sure didn't want that. Instead she strolled along beside him as they made their way through a yard full of fat chickens that clucked noisily and pecked at the ground and each other.

"I'll show you my horse," Francie said as they stepped into the barn.

"You have a horse?" Tamara asked, concerned. "But you're too little to ride."

"Oh, Tamara," Francie said disgustedly. "Grandpa gave me Black Beauty on my third birthday, and I rode before that."

Clay chuckled. "I'd think you of all people would be careful about telling a person they were too little to do something. I notice you bristle when anyone tells you that. You must have been about the same size as Francie when you were her age."

A surge of anxiety rendered Tamara momentarily speechless. He was right on both counts, but it was the second one that frightened her. Francie was the same size Tamara had been at seven. Not only that, but the little girl looked almost exactly like Tamara had. The mother-daughter resemblance was striking, and she was going to have to make sure that fact wasn't brought to the attention of any of the Rutledge family.

"You're right," she told Clay as she frantically searched her mind for a different topic, "it was insensitive of me. I'm sorry, Francie, I'm sure you're an excellent horsewoman. You said her name is Black Beauty. Is she all black?"

Clay whooped with laughter, and Francie looked a little sheepish. "Not exactly," she said slowly. "Mommy named her after the Black Beauty in the story."

The amusement drained out of Clay's expression, but he continued to smile. "Black Beauty is a palomino pony."

Apparently that was meant to explain everything, but Tamara had no idea what a palomino looked like. "I'm sorry," she said, "but I'm not at all familiar with horses."

His arm went all the way across her waist and hugged her to a stop in front of a stall. "This is Black Beauty," he said.

She looked, then laughed. The horse was a small, graceful beauty, all right, but she was fawn colored with a blond mane and tail. There wasn't a spot of black on her.

Francie scrambled up the paddock gate and straddled it, then threw her arms around the horse's neck. "Hello, Black Beauty," she greeted enthusiastically. "I've missed you, but I brought you a treat. See." She put her hand under the horse's nose and opened her fist to reveal two sugar cubes, which Black Beauty promptly devoured. Francie giggled, then turned her head to face her father. "Can we go riding, Daddy? Please. I haven't ridden her for so long. See, she wants to go for a run."

Clay looked at Tamara. "Well . . . I don't know, honey. Tamara's never ridden a horse. . . ."

Tamara swallowed with dismay at the very idea of trying to stay astride one of those beasts as it galloped over the plains, but Francie dismissed Clay's concern with a breezy "Oh, it's easy. She'll love it, won't you, Tamara?" It wasn't even a question. "She can ride Lightning. He doesn't go very fast."

Tamara's heart nearly stopped beating. *Lightning.* No way was she going to get on a horse named Lightning, even if this family did have a penchant for misnaming their animals.

She was all set to say so when Clay intervened. "Lightning used to be a spirited gelding, but now he's old and tame and lazy. You'll be lucky if you can get him to trot."

Tamara shivered. "I don't want him to trot. *Amble* is more my speed."

Lightning proved to be a pretty animal, dark brown with a white blaze on his forehead, who nuzzled Tamara when she petted him and nibbled sugar cubes from her hand. Clay saddled him, and after a little persuasion, she let him help her mount. "See, the old boy's as gentle as a lamb," Clay commented as she clung to the saddle horn.

He led the horse around the barnyard, all the while reassuring her. It seemed to her that she was a long way from the ground if she should fall, but she rapidly became more confident and comfortable.

When her fear had mostly abated, he handed her the reins and gave her some rudimentary instructions on how to get Lightning to move, speed up, slow down and stop. It was actually fun, and gave her a sense of invincibility to be able to control this big and powerful animal.

"Will you be all right now while Francie and I go back in the barn and saddle up our horses?" he asked when she came back to him after a short walk outside the yard.

Tamara's fear had been completely replaced by a mood swing in the other direction. The freedom of sitting astride the horse as he moved briskly at her command while the breeze fanned her face and ruffled her hair elated her and stifled her innate caution. "I'll be fine," she said happily. "Lightning and I will just take a turn around the pasture while we're waiting."

Clay's smile dimmed a little. "Okay, but don't go out of sight of the barn," he warned. "We'll just be a few minutes."

Lightning seemed to know what Tamara wanted even before she gave the proper signals, and he cantered across the pasture picking up speed gradually until they were advancing at a brisk trot. The experience was exhilarating. The powerful muscles of the animal moving in an ancient rhythm beneath her gave her a sense of oneness with the steed. She felt as if she'd been released from her earthly ties and could fly.

She was thoroughly enjoying herself as the scenery whizzed by when she heard someone shout her name. Without thinking, she looked back over her shoulder, and in so doing pulled sharply on the reins. The horse rose on his hind legs, and she went soaring through the air into pain and darkness.

Clay watched in horror as Lightning reared to a stop and Tamara was thrown violently to the ground. Dear God, when he'd come out of the barn and seen her disappearing into the landscape on the fast-moving horse, he'd shouted to Francie to stay there, then galloped to Tamara's rescue. He hadn't anticipated that he'd startle her or that she'd jerk on the reins like that.

After quickly bringing his own mount to a halt, he jumped off and ran to where she lay crumpled on the rock-hard earth. He stumbled to his knees beside her and froze. For one horrible moment, it was Alicia he saw lying there. "Noooo!" It was an involuntary wail, torn from deep inside him, but, although it effectively snapped him out of the hallucination, it didn't lessen his panic.

"Tamara," he groaned through dry lips. He reached out and carefully turned her over. Her heart was beating, but she didn't seem to be breathing!

She'd had the breath knocked out of her, and she was unconscious. Quickly he tipped her head back, then forced her mouth open and swabbed her throat with his finger to make sure it was clear. He pinched her nose shut and took a deep breath. Positioning his open mouth over hers to make a leakproof seal, he blew into it until he saw her chest rise, then repeated the procedure several times until she started breathing on her own.

With an involuntary sob of relief he gathered her limp body in his arms and cradled her to him as he rocked back and forth murmuring frantically, "Tamara! Honey, wake up. Open your eyes. You're all right. You've got to be." He could feel her heart beating evenly against him, but she was still unconscious. "Sweetheart, look at me," he pleaded. "I can't lose you, too!"

He kissed her closed eyes, her scrapped and dirt-smeared cheeks, then nuzzled the soft hollows at the sides of her neck and trailed kisses down her throat. Clay was aware of what he was doing but he couldn't stop. If she were badly hurt he'd never forgive himself. He shouldn't have allowed her on that horse!

Then she moved. A barely discernible shifting at first, but then slowly her arms came up and around his neck as her eyelids fluttered open. Her face was only an inch or so below his, and he could feel her sweet, cool breath on his chin and see the confusion in her magnificent deep brown eyes. "Clay. What...? How...?" It was no more than a whisper, but at least she was conscious and knew him.

"I'm here, love." His own voice shook, and his arms around her tightened as his mouth lowered to hers once more. The action was not to save her life this time, but to ease his own aching need to absorb her into himself—spiritually and mentally as well as physically.

Her lips moved under his and parted, allowing him the intimacy he craved. She was so soft and cuddly and responsive, and even in this acrid environment the floral fragrance of potpourri surrounded her. He lost track of everything but the embrace and the kiss they were sharing. Her willingness surprised him. He'd thought his tormenting desire was one-sided, but what amazed him even more was her obvious inexperience.

Not that her caresses were disappointing—far from it. But the unsure hesitancy of them set his pulse hammering. She didn't even know how to deepen a kiss, but her fumbling attempts to follow his lead in mating her tongue with his were more endearing than anything he'd ever experienced. Even with Alicia.

Alicia. His muscles tightened with guilt. What was he thinking of? He shouldn't be making love with this naive young woman. He had a wife. Alicia would always be alive in his heart. He had to stop this right now, but although his conscience protested, the rest of him was totally centered on the woman in his arms. Tamara, who had melted the yearlong frost that had frozen his psyche, was now rapidly setting him on fire. The best he could manage was to slow down and teach her how to drive him even further over the edge with her moist, warm tongue and her sharp little teeth.

The blood pounding in his ears shut out the sound of hammering hooves until it was too late to avoid the embarrassment of being caught in a romantic embrace by Francie, the last person he wanted to see him kissing a woman who wasn't her mother.

The little girl reined Black Beauty to a stop. "Daddy, did Tamara fall off the horse? Is she hurt?"

Tamara was equally startled, and she tried to pull away. Clay had every intention of releasing her, but his arms tightened instead of loosening. He couldn't let her go. Not yet. She didn't seem to mind, but relaxed against him again while he reassured the child. "Yes, Tamara did fall. She doesn't seem to be hurt except for scratches and bruises, but what are you doing out here, young lady? I told you not to leave the yard until I came back."

Now that he'd brought up the subject, he remembered that he was upset with Tamara, too. A surge of anger finally broke the spell that had mesmerized them, and he clasped her arms and held her away from him. "And you," he said grimly, "I seem to remember telling you the same thing. So why were you tearing off across the meadow? Did Lightning run away with you?"

She shook her head and her eyes filled with tears. "No. I'm sorry. I was enjoying the ride so much that I lost track of how far we'd gone."

She broke off with a sob and jarred loose more of his self-control. "Don't cry," he murmured hoarsely and gathered her back into his embrace. "Oh, God, Tamara, I can't stand it if you cry."

She buried her bruised face in his shoulder, but there were no more sobs and he was content just to hold her again.

When he was reasonably sure his voice wouldn't shake, he spoke to Francie, who also looked contrite. "I'm sorry, baby. I didn't mean to speak so harshly, but you must understand that when you're on a horse you're to follow my instructions at all times. Otherwise I can't let you ride.''

"But, Daddy, you were gone so long. I was afraid you'd both gotten lost or thrown.''

Clay knew she was right. It was his fault more than hers. He shouldn't have spent all that time caressing Tamara. He should have taken her back to the ranch immediately, instead of acting like a randy teenager with his first girl. Damn. Now what was he going to do? He'd obviously have to send her away.

That thought brought a jab of pain, and a low moan escaped from deep within him as his arms again tightened around her. "I'm sorry you were upset," he said to Francie, "but just remember what I said. Now, I want you to ride back to the ranch and tell Grandma what happened. Ask her to send someone out here with the Jeep to take Tamara to the house.''

Tamara raised her head and shook it. "No, I want to ride Lightning back.''

Clay stared at her in amazement. "No way," he bellowed. "I'm not putting you on a horse again.''

"But I've got to, don't you see? I like riding, and I don't want to be afraid, but I will be if I don't get right back on Lightning. It was my fault I fell, not his.''

He knew her logic was right on, but he still wasn't going to allow her to do it. "I'm sorry, honey, but we don't know yet how badly you've been hurt. You were unconscious—''

"Only for a few minutes," she interrupted.

"That's all it takes to indicate a head injury. You could black out again at any time.''

"But, Clay, I'm all right. I'll show you," she insisted as she uncurled herself from him and stood, only to sway dizzily. She would have fallen if he hadn't jumped up and caught her.

"That does it," he grated. "You're not riding back to the ranch alone, but if you feel up to it, you can ride with me on Wind Dancer."

She looked over at the sleek ebony stallion and blinked. "Wind Dancer?"

He managed a weak grin. "Yeah. When you ride him, it's like dancing on the wind."

She chuckled. "He's the one who should have been named Black Beauty."

He was relieved that she was able to react quickly enough to banter with him. That seemed to indicate that there was no serious damage to her lovely head. "I can see why you took up teaching," he groused teasingly. "Your mind works only with facts and logic."

Before she could reply, he picked her up and carried her over to his horse. She was as light as a child. He lifted her into the saddle and handed her the reins before mounting behind her.

"You ride up ahead, Francie," he instructed his daughter, "but take it easy. Don't go faster than a trot."

"What about Lightning?" Tamara inquired. "How will he get back?"

"He'll follow us," Clay said as he reached around her and took the reins.

When the animal started to walk, the sudden movement rocked Tamara back against Clay's chest and belly. He put one arm around her waist to hold her there and she relaxed against him with her head on his shoulder. It was the most erotic horseback ride he'd ever taken, with her bouncing along the length of his torso to the rhythm of the stallion.

Of its own volition, his palm slid up to cup the underside of her high, firm breast. She caught her breath and he quickly moved his hand back to her waist. "Sorry," he murmured, afraid he'd offended her, but she turned her head and brushed her lips against his throat.

His heart bucked with excitement and he rubbed his chee
in her hair. It was all he could do not to change direction an
race the wind to a secluded hideaway he knew, where h
could have Tamara all to himself and make love to her th
way he longed to. First hot, fast and explosive to appease th
raw need. Then later, slow and sweet and immensely fulfil
ing until they were both sated.

A beautiful, erotic dream, but only a dream. It woul
never happen. *Could* never happen. They only had the re
of this day together, and even then never alone. Tomorro
he would apologize for his weakness and send her home t
Iowa and the classroom full of second-grade kids wh
needed her.

But, dammit, he needed her, too.

He needed her bright smile across the breakfast table fro
him in the mornings, and her warm welcome when he cam
home in the late afternoons. He needed her to give his sma
motherless daughter the tender loving care that she lav
ished so willingly on Francie. He needed her to preside ov
his home—

Oh, hell, who did he think he was kidding? *He needed h
to lavish some of that loving care on him!*

He needed her company in the long, lonely evenings, h
warmth, her touch, her tenderness. He needed her arn
around him, her kisses, her sweet responsiveness. He neede
her for sex, dammit, and that's the one thing he couldn
take from her, even if she wanted it, too. He couldn't tak
all the things he needed from her without giving her wh
she needed from him, and it was impossible for him to d
that.

Tamara was a very open person. She didn't attempt t
conceal her emotions, and he'd gotten to know her we
during the short time she'd been living in his house. Sh
could never be happy with a husband who didn't love he
and love was about the only thing he couldn't give her.

He liked her. No, it went deeper than that. He cared strongly for her. But Alicia would always be his love, his wife, his soul mate. He could never again think of himself as an honorable man if he selfishly deprived Tamara of the chance to find a man who would love her the way she deserved to be loved.

Chapter Six

Tamara's fall caused quite a commotion back at the ranc house. However, after she'd showered and applied a disin fectant to the scratches on her face, hands and arms whil Ruth and Juanita laundered her dirty clothes, she was litt the worse for the experience physically and very much be ter emotionally.

The short time between hitting the ground and then wal ing up in Clay's frantic embrace was still a blank, but whe he'd kissed her, she'd been sure she'd died and gone t heaven. Cliché or not, that was the truth.

She hadn't tried to rationalize it; she'd just wound he arms around him and kissed back. Now he was hoverin over her like a concerned lover, and she let herself believe h was.

They were sitting close together on the porch swing, thei thighs touching and their hands clasped, when the fron door opened and a big burly man stepped out. He was ta and barrel chested with a belly that hung over his faded

ow-riding jeans. He, too, wore the mandatory cowboy hat,
nd his boots were worn but no doubt comfortable.

Clay dropped her hand and stood up. "Dad," he said,
"did you get all the fences mended?"

They covered the space between them and embraced be-
ore pounding each other on the back. "You're kidding,
ight?" said the older man with a grin. "No rancher ever has
ll his fences mended. You get one section fixed, and an-
ther one falls apart."

They both laughed, and Clay turned back to Tamara,
who also stood. "Dad, this is Tamara Houston. Tamara, my
ather, Walter."

Tamara put out her hand, and it was quickly swallowed
p in the man's big, work-roughened one. "I'm so pleased
o meet you, Mr. Rutledge," she said shyly. Clay's father
was an intimidating giant with a loud, booming voice and a
rip that could easily break the small bones in her hand.

But his smile was wide and genuine. "Call me Bud. Ev-
rybody does. Hey, it's about time that son of mine brought
ou out to meet us. He says you're a schoolteacher from
owa?"

He was warm and friendly, and Tamara liked him. "Yes,
am." She went on to explain how she happened to be
pending the summer in San Antonio working for his son.
eaving out, of course, the deep, unspeakable secret that she
vas Francie's birth mother and had come to Texas looking
or her. "It was such a wonderful way to get acquainted with
n unfamiliar city and earn extra money, too, that I snatched
p Clay's offer before he could retract it," she finished.

"There was never any chance of that," Clay said, but she
oticed that his mood had sobered and wondered why.
"She's everything I could ask for in a nanny and a house-
eeper. I'm just sorry we can't keep her."

He sounded as if her departure was imminent instead of
vo months away. Was it possible that he really would like
er to take the job full-time? If so, all he had to do was ask.

She'd jump at the chance. It would be an impossible dream come true. With room and board as well as the generous salary he was paying her, she'd make almost as much as she could teaching school, *and she'd be able to share in the raising of her daughter.*

And just maybe he'd fall in love with her in spite of his insistence that he could never love any woman but his late wife.

Tamara knew he desired her. He'd even admitted that, and if the way he'd been acting this afternoon was any criterion, he cared about her well-being. He'd even lost that fierce control he'd been displaying ever since that kiss they'd shared in the car, and this time their kisses had been hot and urgent.

The arrival of more people jarred her out of her fantasizing and brought her down to earth. This time it was Clay's younger brother and his pretty blond wife.

"Hey, guy, where you been keepin' yourself," Dusty asked Clay as they jabbed fists playfully at one another. "Haven't seen you since the family get-together on Mother's Day." He backed off a little to look at Tamara. "And this must be Tamara. You didn't tell me she was young and beautiful." He put out his hand. "Hi, there. I'm Dusty and this is Linda, my wife, who's going to present me with a son in about another month."

Tamara had noticed as they came up the walk that the woman was pregnant. She couldn't help laughing at Dusty's introduction. "Do you know it's a boy or are you just hoping?"

The couple laughed, too, and Linda answered. "We know for sure. I've had an ultrasound that left no doubt about her gender." She blushed prettily.

Just then Francie came running out the door slamming behind her, and threw herself at her uncle. Dusty, who was as tall as his father but slim and lanky, swooped her up in his arms. "There's my sweetie," he said heartily and gave her a big hug. "You still lookin' forward to havin' a new baby cousin?"

"Is he here yet?" Francie asked, bubbling with excitement.

"Not yet, but it won't be long now," Dusty said as he put Francie down. "Go give Aunt Linda a kiss and maybe she'll let you feel him kick."

Francie ran over to Linda, who had lowered herself awkwardly onto one of the padded white rattan chairs, and put her arms around her neck to give her a big kiss. "Does the baby really kick?" she asked her aunt.

"He sure does," Linda said as she took the child's hand and placed it on her distended abdomen. "Feel."

Francie's face lit up and she gave a little squeal of delight. "He kicked my hand," she said with a touch of wonder. "When's he coming out?"

Tamara was surprised but pleased at the casual way they talked about this pregnancy with a child as young as Francie. Her own parents had never discussed childbearing with her, ever. What little knowledge she'd had was imparted by other kids, and that was a mishmash of a few facts and a lot of fantasy.

"In about four more weeks," Linda said in answer to the child's question. "Until then he's growing and getting stronger, because being born takes a lot of strength."

Francie looked up at Tamara. "I wasn't borned. I was chosen," she said with a touch of pride.

Tamara was stunned. "What did you say?"

Clay quickly took over. He sat back down on the swing, then picked up his daughter and put her on his lap. "No, Francie, that's not the way it happened," he said gently. "Remember what Mommy and I told you? You were born the same as all babies are, but not to Mommy. The lady who bore you couldn't take care of you, but she loved you very much and wanted only the best for you, so she put you up for adoption. That's when Mommy and I chose you to be our little girl.''

Tamara fought to hold back the tears that threatened to overwhelm her. What wonderfully compassionate people Clay and his Alicia were. They'd allowed Francie to think kindly of her birth mother. Of *her*.

One of the things that had always tormented Tamara was the fear that her daughter would grow up thinking her real mother hadn't loved or wanted her. Tamara had agonized over that possibility and what it might do to the child's self-image. She'd studied a lot of psychology in her teaching courses and knew the damage that a parent's rejection of a child could cause.

Not that she'd rejected her baby. She'd loved it so much, and wanted it so badly. But she'd been little more than a child herself, still in school and under the care and influence of her own parents. She couldn't even have supported herself, let alone a tiny daughter, and her parents had made it clear that she couldn't come back home if she brought the baby with her.

Lost in her thoughts, Tamara had wandered away from the others and was leaning against one of the posts that supported the porch railing when Clay appeared beside her. "Tamara, do you want me to take you back to San Antonio?" he asked anxiously. "I think you should see a doctor. You don't look well. You're quite pale, and I know from experience that a fall from a horse causes a lot of aches and pains, even if there aren't any broken bones."

She turned to face him and smiled. "It's awfully sweet of you to be concerned about me, Clay. I'm all right, just a little stiff and sore. I'd rather stay here."

He ran one finger slowly down the side of her face. "I'm not sweet, I'm worried," he protested. "I couldn't bear it if anything happened to you, too."

Her, too? So he was thinking of Alicia and her dreadful accident. Tamara's fall and momentary unconsciousness had brought it all back to him, and he was reacting to that horror rather than to any blossoming tenderness for her. Her disappointment was sharp, but she had only herself to blame. He'd been almost brutally honest about his disinterest in a romantic relationship with her or anyone else. She'd let her sexual fantasies run rampant over her good sense.

She blinked in hopes of banishing any trace of the sorrow that may have shown in her eyes, and moved her head so that his fingers fell away from her cheek. "I appreciate your concern, but I've really been looking forward to a good old-fashioned Texas-style barbecue with your family, and I'm not going to let a little tumble ruin it." She was relieved that her voice was strong and steady and revealed none of her inner turmoil.

Clay looked somewhat baffled but nodded. "Okay, if you're sure, but I want you to promise to tell me if you change your mind later."

Tamara promised, and then they were interrupted by more family arriving. This time the man had to be Clay's older brother because he looked so much like their father. With him was a full-figured woman with dark brown shoulder-length hair and brown eyes framed by tortoise-shell glasses. They were accompanied by two teenage boys.

Clay greeted them as boisterously as he had Dusty and Linda, then introduced her. "Tamara, this big lug is my brother, Jim, his wife, Kathy, and their sons, Jim, Jr. and Scott. Guys, meet Tamara Houston. You already know who she is."

Jim Senior's eyes widened. "*This is Tamara?* But she doesn't look any older than Jimmy."

Tamara was getting really tired of that reaction, and she could tell from the look on Clay's face that he was, too. "Well, obviously she is or she couldn't have finished college and spent the past two years teaching," he said, his tone rough with exasperation.

Jim must have caught it, too, because he looked contrite and hastily backed down. "Yeah. Right. Sorry, Tamara," he said and put out his hand to grasp hers. "Don't pay much attention to anything I say. I'm the outspoken member of the family. Ask anyone." He gestured to the others assembled on the porch and they all nodded vigorously in agreement. "They'll tell you that I walk around most of the time with my foot in my mouth."

Tamara took pity on him and smiled as she squeezed his hand. "Don't apologize, Jim," she said cheerfully. "Once they get out of their teens, women like to be thought of as younger than they are."

"Thanks," he said, and she heard the relief in his tone. "All I meant was that I never had a teacher who looked like you when I was a kid."

Everyone laughed and the tension was broken.

Soon Tamara truly felt like one of the family. She helped the women warm casseroles, toss salad and slice long loaves of French bread, which they spread with garlic butter and heated in the oven. When everything was ready, they set it all on the banquet-size folding table that the men had put up on the Mexican-tile patio before they'd started barbecuing steaks and chicken over the big open brick grill.

As she worked, Tamara learned a lot about the Rutledge family from their conversations. For one thing, Jim and Dusty and their families lived in homes of their own on the ranch property. Kathy was a homemaker, as was Ruth, but Linda was an accountant and worked as bookkeeper and tax expert for a real-estate firm in the nearest town.

Much to Tamara's disappointment none of them mentioned Clay's late wife, or the circumstances surrounding Francie's adoption. She kept hoping they would, but didn't feel free to ask questions.

She was thankful, however, that the adoption had been discussed by Clay in her presence. Now she wouldn't have to be so careful that she didn't give away the fact that she knew Francie wasn't Clay's natural daughter. It also presented the possibility that, as they continued to live in the same house and came to know each other better, she could question him about it without arousing his suspicions. He was extremely protective of his child.

Later in the afternoon, after they'd finished eating, the women cleaned up and did the dishes while the men retired to the den to watch baseball on the big-screen television. Francie and her two older cousins went horseback riding.

It had been a wonderfully happy day for Tamara. Even the throbbing soreness from the fall couldn't dampen her spirits. She'd never experienced the camaraderie of a big family gathering before. Her grandparents had all died while she was still very young, and she had no aunts, uncles or cousins. Family holidays had never been special for her parents and her, and she hadn't known what she was missing until now. Clay's close-knit family had accepted her into the fold without reservation, and she wondered if he knew how lucky he was to have them.

When the dishes were done and the kitchen restored to its former pristine condition, the women scattered in different directions. Tamara was still a little uneasy about Francie going off on horseback with her cousins, although Clay and the others had assured her that this happened often and the boys would take good care of her.

Nevertheless, Tamara decided to take a walk and watch for their return. She slipped out the back door and headed across the barnyard. After stooping to pick up a fluffy kitten that was following her, she carried it while she strolled. When she came to the barn, she veered off course and entered it to see if possibly the kids had come back and were inside grooming their horses. There was no sign of them, but as she neared the tack room she heard male voices.

Thinking it might be the two boys, she stopped short of the open door and listened. " ... she's great with Francie," said the voice she recognized as Clay's.

"Sure she is," allowed the other voice, Jim's. "I can see that for myself, but dammit, man, what are your neighbors going to think? For that matter, you must know what conclusions your whole circle of friends is going to draw."

They were talking about her. Tamara moved closer.

"I don't care what they think!" Clay countered.

"Obviously not." Jim's tone was sarcastic. "But you'd better start caring. That little gal is gorgeous, and sexy as hell. Even an old married man like me can see that, so don't try my patience with a song and dance about how you haven't noticed. Having her living in your house is going to cause a lot of talk, if it hasn't already done so."

Tamara gasped as surprise was replaced with searing disappointment. Apparently she hadn't been as accepted into this family as she'd hoped. But they'd been so nice, and so friendly. Was it only good manners instead of approval?

"I don't intend to defend myself to you about anything," Clay said angrily. "Frankly, it's none of your damn business."

Tamara pressed her fists to her mouth to keep from crying out. She wouldn't want Clay to quarrel with his brother about her even if Jim was wrong about this, and she suspected that he was only too right. But neither could she do the decent thing and rectify the situation by resigning and going back to Iowa. She'd do anything she had to in order to spend this one summer with her precious little girl.

She was jolted out of her pondering by Jim's raised voice. "The hell it's not! Don't forget, Texas is still part of the Bible Belt, and people here aren't as open-minded as those in other parts of the country. But it's not only your reputation I'm concerned about. Tamara will be the one most tarnished. The woman always is. And what about Francie? Do you want her little friends to taunt her about her daddy's live-in girlfriend?"

"You bastard!" Clay thundered amid sounds of scuffling.

Tamara stood frozen to the spot, unable to decide whether to make herself known and try to stop them, or run away and pretend she'd heard nothing.

Before she could act, the scuffling stopped, leaving only the sound of heavy breathing. "Hell, boy, when you gonna learn not to take a swing at me?" Jim grumbled. "I'm bigger than you are. Now, you gonna settle down so I can let you go?"

For a moment she heard only panting, then Clay answered, "Yeah, I guess so, but you better watch your mouth."

If Tamara was translating the sounds correctly, Jim had apparently been restraining Clay and now turned him loose. "I'm only telling you like it is," Jim assured him. "From now on the ball's in your court." She heard the sound of boots on the wooden floor. "Come take a look at our new bull. He's a beauty."

That was Tamara's signal to get out of there before she was caught eavesdropping, but the conversation left her uneasy. Would Clay come around to Jim's way of thinking? If he did, could she convince him otherwise?

The rest of the day flew by, and it was late before Clay, Tamara and Francie got back to San Antonio. The disturbing conversation with Jim had niggled at Clay all afternoon, and he knew that his brother was right. It just gave him that much more reason to send Tamara away, but God, how he hated the thought. He'd miss her, he couldn't deny that. But more importantly, she was a great housekeeper and so good with Francie.

He'd intended to talk to her about the situation tonight, but by the time they got home she looked so tired and washed out that he insisted she take a long hot soak in the bathtub and then go to bed while he supervised Francie's shower and tucked her in.

He'd been an insensitive clod. Tamara had taken a bad fall. He should have brought her back to the city right away and taken her to the hospital for a thorough checkup.

As he kissed Francie good-night and turned off the lamp beside her bed, he vowed to talk to Tamara tomorrow and tell her this arrangement wasn't going to work.

Clay awoke the following morning with a heavy heart and a stubborn determination to tell Tamara she'd have to leave. He'd even break down and confess that it was because he was too attracted to her and couldn't trust his tenuous self-control, although few hot-blooded Texas males would admit to such a humiliating weakness.

He dressed quickly and hurried down the stairs so he could get this over with before he could talk himself out of it, but halfway down he heard a crash from the kitchen. Startled, he ran down the remaining steps calling her name. In the kitchen, he found her crouched over a pile of broken crockery on the floor, sobbing. "Tamara, what happened? Did you cut yourself?" He knelt on the floor beside her and cupped her shoulders. "Honey, look at me. Are you hurt?" His voice trembled with anxiety.

She raised her head to look at him, and there were tears streaming down her face. With a groan, he pulled her close and held her. She winced when he first touched her, but then melted into his embrace and continued sobbing.

The soft, slippery material beneath his palms had a sensuous texture that aroused unruly male urges, and he realized that she was wearing a blue satin robe that had fallen open from her knees down to reveal a nightgown of the same color. He hadn't seen her less than fully dressed before. She'd never appeared downstairs in her nightclothes, and a twinge of alarm tugged at him. Was she ill? Had she been hurt worse than she'd admitted in that fall yesterday?

He held her more tightly, and her closeness eased the ache of emptiness that had tormented him ever since he'd reluctantly handed her over to his mother after the accident yesterday morning. He patted her gently and murmured words of endearment, knowing he shouldn't but unable to restrain himself. Hell, he couldn't very well haul her to her feet and fire her when she was obviously so miserable and possibly injured, as well.

"It's all right," he comforted her. "Go ahead and cry if it makes you feel better, but tell me, did you hurt yourself?"

She shook her head against his shoulder. "No. Not today."

That wasn't exactly a reassuring answer. "What do you mean by 'not today'?"

"I . . . I mean, my muscles feel like that horse had . . . had trampled on me yesterday instead of just th-throwing me," she stammered between sobs. "And . . . and now I've bro-broken your pretty dishes. I'm s-such a klutz. I can't do anything right!"

She started to wail again, but Clay almost laughed with relief as he trailed kisses in her silky hair. "Those dishes are replaceable, and you're not a klutz," he assured her. "Your muscles are bruised and stiff from that fall yesterday. It's to be expected. You shouldn't even be out of bed."

She snuggled closer. "But I have to get breakfast for you and Francie."

"Francie and I can get our own breakfast," he said gruffly. "Let me help you up. I'm going to put you back to bed and rub you down with a good strong liniment to unknot those muscles. If you're not allergic to aspirin I have extra-strength tablets that will help relieve the pain. You'll feel better by tomorrow."

"Tomorrow!" Tamara moaned. "But I've got to take care of Francie today."

"I'll take her to the office with me," he said in his best no-argument tone. "There's an extra room in my suite that we've fixed up as an employee lounge. There's a television in there, and she can take whatever toys or games she wants to entertain herself with. She won't mind. She's done it before."

Tamara continued to protest, but Clay finally managed to muster enough self-control to put her away from him and stand. He reached down and lifted her carefully to her feet.

"Watch out for the broken dishes," he warned, then lifted her up, carried her upstairs and put her back to bed. "I'm going to wake Francie, tell her to get dressed and pick whatever toys she wants to take with her," he told Tamara. "Then I'll be back to give you a rubdown."

Her only reply was a muttered okay, and he knew it hadn't occurred to her yet that in order to rub her down he'd have to remove her clothes. Just the thought of it made him shiver.

By the time he returned with a tube of ointment, which he'd warmed in hot water, several large clean towels and a bottle of aspirin, he found Tamara lying on her back with her eyes closed. As he approached, she opened them. They were blurred with pain and tears, but she was no longer sobbing. The poor kid had really taken a beating, both physically and emotionally, when Lightning threw her. Clay felt guilty and miserable. If he hadn't scared her, the horse would never have reared.

He took a deep breath and smiled as he sat down on the side of the bed. "Tamara, in order to do this properly you're going to have to take off your robe and gown," he said in his most professional tone.

Her eyes widened. "You mean you..." Her voice trailed off.

"Don't forget I'm not only a medical man, but I was raised on a ranch," he said reassuringly. "I'm an old hand at massaging the kinks out of muscles that are all knotted up after a fall from a horse."

Tamara blushed, and that in itself was a powerful turn on, but it also helped to shore up his self-control. No way was he going to do anything to disillusion her.

"I...I don't think I can raise my arms enough to pull off my nightie," she said shyly.

"That's all right. I'll do it." Her eyes widened but he ignored her reaction. "Now, let me help you get up and out of that robe."

He threw the lightweight cover back, and she groaned as she rolled off the bed, then clung to him while he assisted her to stand. She had her back to him, and he waited for her to untie the sash of the robe, then slipped it off her shoulders and arms and tossed it across the foot of the bed. Her arms were badly bruised.

"Okay, now I'm going to take off your nightgown. Then I want you to climb back into bed and lie on your stomach."

She gave a curt nod. "All right."

Fortunately the gown was loose fitting. He was able to slip it off her shoulders, as well, and let it fall to the floor, but he was unable to stifle a gasp at what he saw. Her creamy skin was blotched with nasty purple and black bruises. A surge of protective tenderness shook him, and he had to fight a powerful desire to trail kisses over her poor, battered body and make it all well again.

In deference to her modesty he handed her a towel to drape over her front, and she crawled back into bed as he'd instructed. He quickly pulled the sheet up to her waist. "That's right," he said encouragingly. "See, that wasn't so bad, was it?"

He continued the light banter while he removed the top from the tube of ointment and squeezed a generous amount into his palms, gratified to note that his hands weren't trembling. He didn't dare let himself think about the smoothness of her skin or the softness of her flesh as he gently massaged her upper back. Instead he concentrated on the tortured sinews underneath and the painful contusions that marred the otherwise blemish-free perfection. No wonder she could hardly move.

Tamara sighed with pure pleasure as Clay's strong, smooth hands worked magic on her aching muscles. She'd awakened this morning so stiff and taut that every movement was agony. She'd hoped she could hide her discomfort from him until he left for work, but it had been all she could do to struggle into her robe and stumble downstairs. Even her hands were so cramped and raw from pulling on the reins that she couldn't hold on to the dishes, and had shattered them along with her precarious control.

Slowly her muscles began to relax, and she seemed to sink more comfortably into the mattress. His fingers were firm but gentle in their manipulation, releasing strain and coaxing out the soreness.

Within a few minutes, she was floating in a dreamlike state, and by the time he stopped and pulled the sheet and blanket over her again, she had drifted into a somnolent trance. She assumed she was dreaming when she felt his feather-light kiss on her cheek and heard him murmur softly, "Sleep tight, sweetheart."

Chapter Seven

For the next three days, Clay kept solemnly reminding himself that as soon as Tamara had recovered from that fall he was going to send her back to Iowa. He even composed the speech in his mind, then kept refining it by adding a sentence here, subtracting a word there—rather like probing a sore tooth with his tongue. He only succeeded in confusing his motives even more and prolonging the agony.

He couldn't bear the thought of hurting her feelings or making her think he didn't want her, didn't need her. But neither could he admit that it was because he *did* want and need her so desperately that he was sending her away.

Dammit, how had he gotten himself into this situation? It was really so simple. He was sexually attracted to her. Nothing so surprising about that. She was a sexy lady, as his brother, Jim, had so crudely pointed out, and Clay had been celibate for a long time.

He and Alicia had been hot-blooded lovers all their married life, and he missed that exciting and necessary release, but Tamara was very young, and an employee, which made her doubly off-limits. The solution was to remove the temptation, and that's what he intended to do, so why was he finding it so difficult?

He wasn't supposed to want her in his life as well as in his bed. There was no reason for him to look forward to coming home to her after a long day at his practice. It was nonsense that the house felt so lonely and deserted when she was away on her days off, and there was no justification for the pure terror he'd felt when he saw her crumpled on the ground.

Those were emotions reserved for a loved one. For an adored wife. For Alicia, not Tamara! He'd experienced all those feelings with Alicia, but Tamara was merely a distraction, an enticement that was driving him crazy. So why did he continue to turn away applicants for her job that the employment office sent to him?

Tamara was becoming more important to him every day, and that could only lead to heartbreak. If he gave in to his craving and took her to bed, it would satisfy his lust, but then the enchantment would be gone. Alicia would still be the love of his life, and he'd be trapped in a relationship with a much younger woman that wouldn't satisfy either of them.

No, it was time to stop procrastinating and end this nonsense, and tonight was the night. Tamara's muscles were no longer so sore, although he still saw her wince when she stretched them. The bruises were fading but still noticeable enough that she hid them by wearing slacks and long sleeves when she went out. Even more importantly, Francie was becoming much too dependent on her.

He ignored the desolation clawing at him at the thought of losing her and forced his mind to zero in on a plan.

During the noon break he called home, and Tamara answered. Her voice was low and sexy even on the telephone, and it was all he could do not to hang up without speaking and leave things as they were. Let nature take its course and then try to repair the damage afterward.

"I'm calling to tell you not to plan on fixing dinner tonight," he said instead. "If you feel up to it, I'd like to take you out to eat."

"I always feel up to eating out," she said, and he heard the sparkle of excitement in her voice, like that of a child who's been promised a special treat.

"Good. I'll make reservations at one of the cafés on the Riverwalk. Is seven okay with you? I should be home by six."

"Seven's fine. Francie and I will be ready when you are."

She caught him by surprise and threw him off guard. "No, no, Tamara. I'll arrange for a baby-sitter to stay with Francie, and I'll bring home their favorite take-out food," he explained. His voice unintentionally dropped to a more intimate tone when he added, "This time it's just you and me."

Damn, that sounded like a come on. A...a date. But that wasn't what he intended. He just wanted to create a pleasant, friendly atmosphere when he told her she'd have to leave, so she wouldn't think she was being summarily dismissed. Fired.

"Really?" she murmured in a breathless whisper, sending shivers of desire down his spine. "That's very... very thoughtful of you. I'll see you around six."

Clay put the receiver back in its cradle and ran his hand over his face. Oh, Lord, now what had he done? Why was it that every time he got near her or heard her voice, his mind turned to mush? He was trying to ease her out of his life, not lead her on.

Now she probably thought he had a personal interest in her, and he didn't. Well, he did, but it was only friendship. A stab of conscience brought him up short. Okay, so his feelings for her were strong and disturbing, but it was strictly sex, not romance.

Why would she even want to go on a date with him? He was old enough to be her uncle, and he'd been married for fourteen years before his wife died. She was probably just impressed with his standing in the community and his moderate wealth.

What she needed was a young stud, and he intended to send her back to Iowa where she no doubt had them flocking around her.

Tamara spent the latter part of the afternoon excitedly getting ready for her date with Clay. She showered and shampooed her hair, then put it up on large rollers to give it body and bounce. After several minutes of rummaging around in her cosmetic case, she found a small tube of face cream, which was touted as doing wonders for the complexion, and lathered it on generously.

Clay had never asked her out before without Francie. Surely that meant he wanted to spend time alone with her, even if it was in the middle of a crowded restaurant. He'd been so attentive since her fall, hovering over her, insisting that she take it easy, and even massaging her still-aching muscles every night.

That last thought sent quivers through her, even though after that first time when he'd applied the liniment, she'd always been fully dressed. He had such gentle hands, and he knew exactly how and where to knead her to drain away the soreness. No professional masseur could have done it more effectively, or more impersonally.

He was a perfect gentleman at those times, which annoyed her somewhat. How could he not be aroused at all while stroking her body when his touch sent prickles of desire racing through her?

Much to her dismay, she'd almost decided he simply wasn't attracted to her, when out of the blue came this telephone call asking her to go out with him. She didn't understand, but neither was she going to question his action. It was a start, and she intended to make the most of it.

She chose to wear a new dress she'd bought here in San Antonio. Styled like a Mexican wedding dress, the garment was made of white crinkly cotton gauze with a scoop neckline and a swirling, three-tiered skirt. She added a silver chain-link belt and silver earrings, but left her throat, and the deep expanse of flesh revealed by the low neckline, bare.

Maybe that would wake up his sleeping libido.

Clay's libido was wide awake and throbbing as he sat across from Tamara at the small linen-covered table outside on the Riverwalk. If Jim thought she was sexy in jeans he should see her tonight. There was nothing girlish about her now. She was all woman, and seductive as hell without even being aware of it.

Or was she aware of it? Was she deliberately trying to drive him out of his mind? If so, she was doing a great job. That white gown she wore highlighted her shining ebony hair, and his fingers itched to run through it and feel the electricity that crackled when she moved her head.

Plus that low neckline was playing havoc with his nervous system. Its dip ended just above the upward slope of her breasts, and every time she moved, he was torn between fear that it would reveal more than she wanted it to, and hope that it would.

In addition to all his other sins, he was rapidly becoming a dirty old man. How in hell was he supposed to engage in amusing small talk when he was about to burst into flame?

Tamara was so pleased and excited by the simple act of his taking her out to dinner that he felt like an unfeeling brute. She'd been positively bubbling all evening. Obviously his plan to tell her in the impersonal setting of an upscale restaurant that he wouldn't be able to employ her for the rest of the summer wasn't going to work.

He couldn't spring that on her now, after she'd enjoyed their unintentional "date" so much. And he had enjoyed it as well. If it hadn't been for the burden of guilt he carried it would have been a perfect outing.

Being with her was such a pleasure. She was sweet and caring and so easy to please. She always said thank-you for each small service or compliment and made him feel good about himself, even now when he knew he would soon turn on her and send her away. That thought was almost unbearably painful, but for that very reason he had to do it tonight. If he waited he feared he wouldn't have the strength to do it at all.

Tamara took the last sip of her coffee and set the cup back in its saucer. She'd been having a marvelous time. The food was delicious, the ambience breathtaking, and the company everything she could ask for.

Well, almost. Clay looked marvelous in his white trousers and navy blazer, and he was attentive, generous and thoughtful. He laughed a little, smiled a lot and really seemed to enjoy her company, but there was one flaw. The sadness was back in his eyes. Sadness that had been so noticeable when she first met him, but had slowly receded since then. Or had it? Had that impression just been wishful thinking? An illusion brought about by her desperate hope that he would exorcise the ghost of his late wife and fall in love with her?

"If you're finished eating, perhaps you'd like to take a stroll along the river," he said, breaking into her disturbing speculations.

"I'd love to," she answered without hesitation. She didn't want this enchanting evening to end, at least not yet.

After Clay settled the bill, they wandered hand in hand down the romantically lighted footpaths and through elegant shops, boutiques, handicraft displays and galleries. By the time they got back to where they'd parked the car, the stores were closing for the night, but the nightclubs and cabarets were just hitting their stride, spilling music—jazz, blues, country and rock—out into the streets in a mellifluous harmony.

On the short drive home, Tamara sighed and leaned her head back against the headrest. "Thank you, Clay," she said dreamily.

He glanced at her out of the corner of his eye. "Thank you for what?"

She smiled. "For the marvelous evening. It was perfect. The food, the setting, exploring all those posh shops."

Although it was too dark in the car to see clearly, she was almost sure he frowned. "I'm afraid I've been selfish and thoughtless," he said. "I should have introduced you to some of the eligible young men here in town, seen that you got out and about more while you're here."

His rather sharp tone as well as his words brought her upright in astonishment. "What are you talking about? I've no desire to be fixed up with a 'young' man." Then a thought struck her, and she was crushed. "I guess you didn't enjoy this evening as much as I did," she said sadly. "I'm sorry. I . . . I didn't realize . . ."

Clay made a small groaning sound and reached for her hand. "That's not what I meant, Tamara." His voice was raspy. "I'm sure I enjoyed the evening a great deal more than you did. Much more than I should have, in fact."

He was saying the right words, but his tone was one of . . . hopelessness?

"Is there some reason why you shouldn't enjoy an evening out with me?" she asked testily. He was talking as if she was unacceptable for some reason, and he shouldn't be involved with her socially.

"Yes, there is," he answered. "I need to talk to you when we get home, Tamara." Before she could respond, he turned into the driveway and stopped. "I have to take the baby-sitter home," he told her, "but I won't be long. Please wait for me in the living room."

Her eyes widened. "The living room?" That room was large and formal and seldom used unless there were visitors. "Don't you mean the library?"

"No, I prefer to use the living room. Maybe you wouldn't mind making a pot of coffee?" He opened his door to get out.

Tamara was swept by a wave of anxiety. What was the matter? Had she done something wrong? He didn't seem angry with her, but she had noticed that he'd been a little preoccupied all evening.

She knew it wouldn't do any good to question him now. Instead, as soon as he left with the baby-sitter, she made the coffee he asked for. She had just set a silver tray on the table in front of the sofa when she heard him come in the front door.

Within seconds, he appeared in the wide archway, and she managed a wobbly smile. "I made the coffee. Would you like me to pour you a cup?"

He walked toward her but didn't return the smile. "Thank you, and yes, please."

She poured and handed him a cup and saucer, then poured her own and sat down on the sofa. Clay joined her. For a moment, neither of them spoke, and the tense atmosphere and unnatural silence made Tamara's skin crawl. Why didn't he just say what he wanted and get it over with?

"Tamara..."

"Clay..."

They both jumped in at once, then withdrew.

"I'm sorry," Clay said. "You first."

She shook her head. "No, you go first. I was only going to ask what you wanted to talk to me about."

He added cream to his coffee, and she noticed that the silver pitcher shook slightly in his hand. He really was nervous about something. He cleared his throat. "It's recently come to my attention that there's talk about our living arrangement."

She blinked. So that was it. He was upset about what Jim had told him. "Yes, I know. I went into the barn Sunday looking for Francie and overheard you and Jim talking," she admitted. "I'm sorry, I should have made myself known, but it took me by surprise and was over so quickly...."

He looked startled but not angry. "Then you're aware of what's being said. It's true, you know. The two of us living together does put us in a compromising position. I should have known better than to ask you to stay, but I hadn't counted on it taking so long to find a permanent housekeeper."

Dear God, was he going to fire her? She heard her cup rattling in its saucer and put it down on the table. On Sunday he'd been indignant when his brother had brought up the subject. After all, they weren't doing anything wrong.

Clay watched Tamara's expression change from inquisitive to apprehensive to defeated. It took all his control not to take her in his arms, beg her to stay with him and say to hell with what the neighbors thought.

She looked up at him, her eyes wide with distress. "Are you asking me to leave?"

"Honey, I...I don't want to lose you," he falteringly admitted, "but I don't seem to have any choice. You must know that I'm...attracted to you, and I don't know how much longer I can resist—" His nerves snapped, and he banged his cup and saucer down on the table and stood. "Dammit, Tamara, I have all the normal male urges, and I want you. Not just in my kitchen, but in my bed!"

He turned his back on her and ran the fingers of one hand through his hair. "You're too young and innocent for that kind of relationship, and I'd never forgive myself if I seduced you into one. Besides, there's Francie to consider. This is her home, and if I ever bring a woman here to live with me in an intimate relationship, she'll be my wife."

His last words echoed in the silence before they dis
solved. Then Tamara's voice, soft with a touch of timidity
sounded behind him. "Then why don't you marry me,
Clay?"

Shock, like a bolt of electricity, immobilized him, and he
just stood there unable to respond. Surely he must have
heard wrong. Why would she want to marry him after he'd
made it plain that he could never love her?

Slowly he turned to look at her, and knew by her expression that he'd heard right. She sat huddled in the corner of
the sofa, her face pink with embarrassment and her eyes
lowered. His heart melted, and he knew he'd have to handle this very carefully.

He hunkered down in front of her, put his fingers under
her chin and lifted her face to meet his gaze. "Why would
you even consider being my wife, Tamara?" he asked gently.

The blush turned from pink to red, but she didn't try to
look away. "Because I . . . I love you."

His heart rate tripled, and he had to take a deep breath
before he could speak again. "That's the nicest thing anyone has said to me in a very long time," he acknowledged
haltingly. "I'm deeply flattered, but don't you think it's
possible that what you feel for me is infatuation rather than
love?" She shook her head, but he hurried blindly on.
"Believe me, honey, I don't mean to trivialize your affec-
tion, but you've known me for such a short time. I suspect
that you feel sorry for me because I'm a widower raising my
child alone, and I know you're fond of Francie—"

"I adore Francie," she interrupted, "but that has nothing to do with my feelings for you."

He wasn't getting through to her, and even worse, the
harder he tried the less he wanted to. She was warm and
loving, and he yearned for the closeness she so generously
offered. Would it really be dastardly of him to take her up
on that offer?

He sighed. Yes, it would be. No matter how much he might wish it were otherwise, he'd have to make more of an effort to convince her that she was misunderstanding her emotions.

Reluctantly he stood and walked a little away from her. As long as he was touching her, he couldn't think straight. "Tamara, have you ever lived with a man before? Other than your father, of course."

That got her attention. "No, I haven't," she snapped.

"All right, then, just think about this for a moment. In the short time you've been here we've been living together in an intimate setting. The three of us have been a family in all but sleeping arrangements. There's also a strong physical attraction between you and me. It's not surprising that all these things have combined to make you think you're in love with me, but you seem to be forgetting one thing."

He paused, for a moment unable to go on. There was no way to put what he had to say that wouldn't seem harsh and insensitive. Then, to his amazement, she said it for him. "You're not in love with me." It was a flat statement spoken without emotion. "I haven't forgotten that, Clay. I won't say it doesn't matter, but I don't see why we couldn't have a happy marriage anyway." She got to her feet and went to stand in front of the fireplace. "I know you're still grieving for the wife you loved so much, but I also know you care about me—"

"Of course I care about you," he hastened to assure her. "I care very deeply, but you deserve much more than that."

"Perhaps I do," she admitted thoughtfully, "but few people get what they think they deserve. As I see it, I can gamble on eventually either finding someone who will play Prince Charming to my Cinderella, or settling for someone who won't be able to offer me as much devotion as you can. I prefer to take my chances on you, and now."

What could he say to that? She seemed to know exactly what she wanted. But could she possibly know how badly he'd be shortchanging her? He knew the sheer joy of sharing mutual, passionate love. Alicia had loved him as much as he'd loved her, and he'd basked in her love. It had radiated from her and warmed him in its glow. He'd never doubted it, and it had brought him happiness and contentment beyond measure.

But he couldn't provide that marital bliss for Tamara because his ability to love so intently had died with Alicia. Did he have the right to deprive Tamara of the opportunity to find a man who could?

"You're tempting me almost beyond my endurance," he told her, "but I have to know that you're aware of what you're agreeing to.

"If I marry again the vows will be the same as the ones I took the first time. *Forever. Till death us do part.* I wouldn't put either Francie or myself through the agony of losing another mother and wife, so unless you want to spend the rest of your life with us, please pack up and go back to Iowa right now and leave us in peace."

She nodded. "Of course it would be forever. I wouldn't have it any other way."

Although she spoke calmly, Clay could see by her expression that she was hurt, and he silently cursed himself for a fool. While only trying to be truthful and make sure she wasn't getting into something she'd regret later, he'd nonetheless been too blunt. His caution snapped. He held out his arms. "Come here, Tamara," he said softly.

She didn't hesitate or argue, but walked into his embrace. He welcomed her warmth and her willingness. There was no holding back with her. She gave him freely of her generous, loving nature and soothed the loneliness that had plagued him so achingly since Alicia's death.

"Forgive me if I sound like I'm bartering for a corporate merger instead of a marriage," he begged. "What I'm trying to say is that you are special to me. I care about you, and

I don't want you to agree to an arrangement you may come to regret."

She put her palms on his chest and pushed back to look up at him. Her expression was one of confusion, but her voice was strong and clear when she spoke. "There's only one thing that needs to be resolved, Clay. I've told you how I feel, so now it's up to you. Do you want me, or don't you?"

With a low groan, he tightened his arms around her and brought her body full-length against his. "Yes, I want you! You came to me at a time when I'd despaired of ever coming to terms with my grief. You've brought light and laughter back into my life, and you've given my daughter the happiness and security she lost when her mother died."

He rubbed his cheek in the silkiness of her hair and smelled the fragrance of crushed rose petals.

"I want you for those reasons, but that's not all. I want to make love with you. I want you to be totally mine. Ours will be a union in the full sense of the word, not a so-called marriage of convenience. In return I promise to cherish and honor you, and be a faithful husband."

Tamara sagged with relief and leaned heavily into the embrace. He didn't disappoint her but wrapped her even more securely in his arms. He lowered his head, and she felt his breath on the side of her neck as his lips moved slowly over the sensitive hollows, trailing shivers in their wake. She kissed his cheek and stroked her fingers through his hair.

She'd taken such a monstrous chance by proposing to him. He could have laughed at her. Or been offended. Never would she have had the nerve to do it if she'd stopped to think about it first, but taking the initiative had never crossed her mind. Not until he'd brought up the possibility of taking a wife as opposed to a mistress. Then the question had just popped out.

He turned his head, and his mouth found hers and clung. It was a sweet blending of lips and tongues and bodies as his

hand moved down to caress her derriere and make her aware
of his arousal. She'd always pulled away before when a man
got that familiar, but this time she welcomed the intimacy
and pressed against him.

"Now you know what you do to me," he whispered
against her ear. "I hope you're not going to insist on a long
engagement."

She shook her head against his chest. "Is four days too
long?"

Clay straightened and held her away from him. "Four
days! But you can't plan a wedding in four days!"

His reaction startled her, and prickles of fear ran up her
spine. Was he already regretting his decision? "Why not?
That is, I don't mean to rush you, but you said—"

His expression of shock softened, as did his tone.
"Honey, it can't be too soon for me, but don't you want to
be married at your home in Iowa? In a long white beaded
dress, with half a dozen attendants and all your family
there?"

No, that's not what she wanted, but was it what *he*
wanted? "My home is here in San Antonio with you now,
Clay," she said tonelessly, "but if you'd rather we had the
ceremony in Iowa..."

He dropped his hands from her shoulders and put an arm
around her waist. "I think we'd better sit down and talk
about this," he said as he led her to the sofa. They sat down
side by side, and again he put his arms around her and drew
her close. "All right, sweetheart, first let's get one thing
straight. I want us to be married as soon as possible, but
surely you want the storybook-type of ceremony with the
showers and the rehearsal dinner and your mother wiping
at tears when your father gives you away?"

Like hell she did. "My father gave me away a long time
ago," she said bitterly, "and my mother's tears were for her
lost dreams, not her lost daughter."

A look of alarm washed over Clay's face, and Tamara knew she was treading on dangerous and forbidden ground. She didn't want to be asked to explain what she'd just said, and hastily attempted to repair the damage.

"What I mean is, my parents and I have been estranged for several years, and I haven't lived in my hometown since I went away to college. I have no other family, but what I'd really like is to have the wedding at . . . that is, if it wouldn't be too much trouble, I'd . . . I'd like for us to be married at your parents' ranch with all your family present," she finished quickly.

Clay hugged her close. "Sweetheart, if you really mean that, I'm relieved and delighted, and Dad and Mom will be, too. I don't like those formal affairs that are more like a stage production than the solemn taking of vows that will bind us for life."

She rubbed her palm over his chest. "Did you and Alicia have a big wedding?"

The question was out before she could bite it back, but Clay didn't seem to mind. "Yes. I argued for a smaller, simpler one, but she wouldn't hear of it. She'd been dreaming of a big, splashy affair all her life, so what could I do but agree?"

Yes, he would have agreed. He was too thoughtful and unselfish to put his own preference ahead of that of the woman he loved. He'd been willing to do it again for her, and he didn't even love her.

Since she'd inadvertently brought up the subject of his first wife, there was another question Tamara needed to have answered, but it was going to be difficult to ask. She took a deep breath and dived in. "Clay, are we going to be able to have babies together?"

She felt him tense, but his voice was calm when he answered. "Is that what you want?"

"I . . . I'd like for us to have more children," she admitted, "but if we . . . that is, if we have to adopt them, it wouldn't matter to me."

She'd been given a second chance to raise her own child. If Clay couldn't give her others, it would be her privilege to take in those who needed a home and loving parents, the way he and his wife had taken in Francie.

Clay relaxed and chuckled. "Oh, I see what you're getting at. You think that because Francie is adopted that you and I can't have children of our own. I'm sorry, love, I should have explained that, but so help me God, I keep forgetting she's not my own flesh and blood."

He settled back and continued. "To the best of my knowledge I'm capable of fathering children, but two years after we were married, Alicia developed a tumor—benign but growing rapidly. There was no choice but to have a partial hysterectomy. She was crushed, but I was so relieved that the problem wasn't life threatening that nothing else mattered."

His voice became huskier as he talked, and Tamara knew it was hard for him to relive that difficult time. How tragic that his beautiful young wife had been forced to sacrifice her ability to have children in order to live, and then had died at too early an age anyway.

"For several years after that, we were busy studying for advanced degrees and then getting started in our professions," he continued, "but once we were settled we started searching for a child to adopt. That's when we found Francie, and she's been a blessing beyond all our hopes. We couldn't have loved a child who'd been born to us more."

Tamara offered a silent prayer of thanks that the baby she'd had to give up had been taken in by this wonderful family who loved her as their own. "Then if it's all right with you, I'd like us to have a few brothers and sisters for Francie," she said shakily.

"I want that very much," he assured her just before he lowered his mouth to hers and taught her the searing ecstasy of erotic kissing.

Later, when the lights were out and Tamara lay in her bed still struggling to tame the unfulfilled desire Clay had aroused in her with his kisses and caresses, her mind returned to their conversation about the adoption of Francie. She didn't want to think about that. It was a subject that was causing her much anguish. Should she tell Clay she was Francie's birth mother? Or should she leave well enough alone and say nothing?

There was no way he could find out unless she confessed. Her parents were the only ones other than herself and Paul Wallace who knew she'd had a baby, and they sure weren't going to tell anybody. She hadn't spoken with her parents since Christmas, and that had been only a short phone call to wish them a happy holiday. A hollow greeting since the conversation had been stilted and cold. Paul Wallace was bound by professional ethics to keep her confidence.

Her mother and father had no idea she'd initiated a search for her daughter, and would be horrified if they learned of it. They didn't even know Tamara was in San Antonio, although tomorrow she'd write a note and tell them she was going to be married.

She rolled onto her side and plumped up her pillow. Was she doing Clay any serious harm by keeping her secret? She didn't see how. She had no great need for Francie to know she was her real mother. All she wanted was the child's love. If her adoptive mother were still alive, that would have been despicable, but Alicia was dead, and Tamara would be giving her daughter the mothering all children needed.

Restlessly she turned onto her other side. She'd almost convinced herself that she wouldn't do any harm by keeping her secret, but how would Clay feel if he somehow found out later what she'd been withholding from him?

She didn't have to wonder; she knew. He'd be furious. He'd consider it an unforgivable betrayal. He'd never go through with the marriage if he found out Tamara had been lying to him, and all three of them would suffer for it. Tamara had so much love to give them both. What would be gained by stirring up a windstorm that could destroy their whole future, when by her keeping quiet they could all live happily ever after?

Rolling over onto her stomach, she buried her head in her folded arms. No, she wasn't going to admit her blood ties to Francie. It was too risky.

This was one instance when Clay was better off not knowing the truth, the whole truth, and nothing but the truth. She'd make sure of that.

Chapter Eight

Sunday morning dawned bright and beautiful at the Rocking R Ranch. Tamara watched the sun come up as she lay in the antique brass bed in a room on the second floor of the ranch house, and shivered with excitement.

Today was her wedding day. In just a few short hours she'd be Mrs. Tamara Rutledge, wife of Clayton and mother of Mary Frances. Never in her wildest dreams had she imagined she'd eventually get her precious daughter back.

Not only that, but Francie had come with a bonus—Clayton Rutledge, the only man she had ever loved, or ever would love. She was doubly blessed. So what if Clay didn't love her. He desired her, and maybe that was even more important. They'd done enough petting in the past few days for her to know that her blood ran as hot as his, and she was eagerly looking forward to consummating their liaison tonight.

She smiled happily. She was terribly inexperienced, but he sensed that and it seemed to please him. He'd teach her how to satisfy him and keep him happy in bed, and when she'd shown him how willing she was to learn, maybe he'd forget that he didn't love her.

Maybe, just maybe, when he realized what a good wife and lover she would be to him, and what a good mother she'd be to his daughter, he'd even let go of the heartbreak of the past and learn to love her.

She was startled out of her daydreams when the door burst open and Francie came running in, still clad in her pajamas, her smile wide and her eyes glowing. "Tamara!" she cried, and leapt onto the bed and into Tamara's arms. "Wake up. Today's the day Daddy and I are going to marry you!"

Tamara sat up and hugged the child, whose little arms were twined around Tamara's neck. "You bet you are, sweetie," she assured her, "and I am awake. I wouldn't miss a minute of this day for anything."

Her cup was running over with happiness. Everything had gone so wonderfully well since she and Clay had announced their engagement. His family was delighted and seemed especially pleased that they wanted to be married at the ranch. And Francie, dear, sweet little Francie. She'd accepted the idea—and Tamara— without hesitation. The first thing she'd said after they'd told her was "Can I walk down the aisle with you?" and the second was "Now can I call you Mommy?"

That second question had almost been Tamara's undoing. She hadn't been sure she could contain the pure joy that threatened to overwhelm her, but Clay had unknowingly defused it to some extent by his answer.

He'd obviously been caught unawares, and his laughter over Francie's first question had been replaced with a frown. It had taken him a minute to answer, and when he did his tone had been bleak. "Well, honey, it's true that Tamara will be your stepmother," he'd said, "but your mother Alicia, will always be your mommy. I think it would be better if you'd just keep on calling Tamara by her name. Okay?''

He'd looked at Tamara then, and she saw the anguished apology in his eyes. Some of the joy had drained out of her. It wasn't easy listening to her daughter call another woman Mommy, but she hadn't let it ruin her happiness. She'd reached out and touched his cheek to let him know it was all right, then she'd looked at Francie and smiled. "There won't be an aisle to walk down," she'd said gently, "but you can be my maid of honor and stand by my side when your daddy and I take our vows.''

That had pleased the child immensely, and she'd started making plans for what she'd wear.

Now the big day was here. Clay, Tamara and Francie had driven down the day before to help decorate the house and prepare for the festivities. The ceremony was set for four o'clock in the afternoon to be followed by the reception and dinner, then the newlyweds would leave Francie with her grandparents and drive to Corpus Christi where they would spend their week-long honeymoon.

Tamara gave Francie a playful swat on the behind, then twisted around so she was sitting on the edge of the bed with her feet on the floor. "Run along and get dressed now, baby," she told Francie. "This is going to be a busy day, and we have to get an early start.''

Francie made a face. "I'm not a baby," she protested.

Tamara looked at her and the corners of her mouth turned up in a sad little smile. "No, you're not, are you? You're growing up so fast." *And I missed the first seven years of your life,* she thought regretfully.

"Are you going to have a baby, like Aunt Linda?" Francie startled Tamara by asking.

"Uh...well, not right away," she stammered, "but your daddy and I hope to have one later. Would you like a little brother or sister?''

"Yeah," she said enthusiastically. "Can I give it a bath and feed it, and take it for a walk in the stroller?"

Tamara laughed. One thing she'd found out about Francie, she wanted everything immediately. "Sure you can, but right now you'd better get dressed. Juanita must be fixing breakfast. I can smell the coffee."

The child scurried out of the room, and Tamara dressed in jeans and a loose-fitting blue denim shirt. She'd just stepped from her room when the door across the hall opened and Clay came out. They nearly collided, and he reached out and circled her with his arms.

"I was going to your room," he said huskily. "Were you by any chance, on your way to mine?"

He looked like a rancher in his jeans and boots, but his shaving lotion had a fragrance of sophistication and virility. She snuggled closer. "I wanted to," she murmured, "but I was afraid it wouldn't be proper. Isn't there some kind of rule about the groom not seeing the bride before the ceremony? I wouldn't want to offend your mother."

His arms tightened. "You can't offend my mother. After living with three sons and a husband, plus numerous ranch hands, she's shockproof, and whoever made up that rule was a sadist. Now, shall we step into one of the bedrooms while I kiss you good-morning, or do you want me to do it right here in the hall?"

The wave of heat that accompanied her memory of his good-night kiss just hours before warned her that they'd better not repeat it in public. "Let's use my room. It has a lock."

He chuckled wickedly and led her in, then closed and locked the door. There was a decided gleam in his eyes when he turned and took her into his arms again. "My beautiful bride," he murmured as his lips roamed over her face, leaving prickles of fire in their wake. "Are you absolutely sure you want to go through with this? You're so young. You have your whole life ahead of you—"

A sharp jab of alarm pierced her and sent shock waves in all directions. "Are you trying to say you want to back out?" Her tone was strident. "That you don't want to marry me after all?"

"No!" he said, hugging her closer. "My God, no! That's not what I'm saying. I'm not sure I could let you go now even if you wanted out, but I can't help feeling . . . I suppose guilty is the proper word. In the short time I've known you, you've given me so much, so willingly. You've banished the loneliness and taught me to enjoy life again instead of just existing, but all you're getting in return is an emotionally damaged middle-aged man and a ready-made family."

She put her fingers to his lips and shook her head. "Don't say that," she pleaded. "Don't even think it. You're not middle-aged, and I love you. Believe me, you've given me much more than you think. More than I could ever repay . . ."

His puzzled expression brought her up short. A few more words and she'd have revealed everything. Maybe it would be wiser for her to go ahead and tell him what she was so afraid to let him know. Was she being deceitful by not confessing that she was Francie's birth mother? Was she being cruel by letting him think he was depriving her of a "normal" marriage when actually he was giving her the one thing no one else could give her? *Her firstborn child.*

"Tamara. What's the matter?"

The alarm in Clay's voice snapped her attention back to him. "N-n-nothing," she stuttered, then looked up at him and grinned, hoping to focus him away from what she'd almost said. "Hey, are you going to give me that kiss you promised or not?"

It worked. His focus was immediately redirected, and when they went downstairs hand in hand a few minutes later, they both were breathless and overheated.

* * *

The hours flew by as the whole family tackled the last-minute finishing touches on decorations and food. At two o'clock, everyone went to their own homes to bathe and dress.

Tamara's nerves started to fray and her stomach filled with butterflies as she stepped out of the shower and wrapped a large towel around her. She wanted to be a beautiful bride for Clay, but she didn't want to remind him of Alicia and his first wedding.

She knew that she looked nothing like his first wife. She was short and Alicia had been tall. She had black hair and Alicia's had been blond. She was fairly pretty, but Alicia had been gorgeous.

Still, all brides tended to look alike, and for that reason she'd decided not to wear a long white dress with a train and veil. Instead she'd chosen a cocktail-length gown of peach lace, and had the florist fashion a wreath of matching peach miniature roses for her headpiece. She'd blow-dried her hair and was applying her makeup when there was a knock at the door, and a voice called, "It's Ruth."

"Just a minute," she replied and hurriedly unknotted the towel and put on her robe before opening the door.

"I don't mean to bother you, dear," Clay's mother said as she stepped into the room, fully dressed and looking lovely. "But Kathy and Jim took Francie home with them so Kathy could dress her, and since your mother isn't here and you have no adult attendants, I thought you might need some help."

Tamara's throat tightened with gratitude, and she blinked a few tears from her eyes. "That's very thoughtful of you, Ruth. I sure could use some assistance. I seem to be all thumbs. As soon as I finish my makeup, I'd appreciate it if you'd help me put on my clothes and fix my hair."

Clay's mother was a handsome woman. A little too hard-angled to be beautiful and too mature to be called pretty, but

n her mauve silk dress accessorized with an amethyst neck-
lace and earrings, she was truly stunning.

At three-thirty, the family returned, and the guests,
friends of the Rutledges who lived and worked in the area,
began to arrive. Tamara sneaked peeks at them out the
window as the cars drove up and people got out. They were
strangers to her, but they were friends of Clay's and she was
eager to meet them. What would they think of her? Would
they feel she was too young for him? Not pretty enough?
The butterflies in her stomach multiplied.

"Don't be nervous," Ruth said from behind her. "It will
be a lovely wedding. We've known these folks, and their
parents and grandparents, all our lives. They think of Clayton as one of their own, and they wish him only the best.
They'll accept you without reservation because you've made
him happy again."

Tamara was warmed by Ruth's quiet words, but she still
had her doubts. "Have I?" she mused, more to herself than
to Ruth.

"Oh, yes," Clay's mother answered. "That's very obvious to all of us. You'd have had to know him for this past
year to truly understand what a difference you've made in
his life. You're the miracle we've all prayed for."

Tamara was too choked up with gratitude to speak. She
wasn't going to cry. If she did, she'd streak the makeup
she'd so painstakingly applied, but her vision was wavy
through the unshed tears. She walked across the room to the
dresser and found a tissue to blot her eyes, then turned back
to face the older woman. "I love Clay with all my heart,"
she said simply.

"I can see that," Ruth agreed. "He loves you, too."

Tamara shook her head. "No, he doesn't. He's fond of
me, but he still grieves for Alicia."

"Of course he grieves for her," Ruth said. "They'd
known each other all their lives, and they'd been married a
long time. But he can grieve for her and still love you."

Tamara had never intended to get into this discussion with anybody, especially Clay's mother, but the woman was s easy to confide in, and Tamara had no one else. "Appar ently he doesn't think so," she said before she could sto herself. "He's told me that he can never love anothe woman the way he loved Alicia."

Ruth's eyes grew round. "He didn't."

Tamara nodded. "Yes, he did. It wasn't his idea for us t get married, Ruth. I proposed to him."

"But he obviously agreed," she observed.

Tamara shrugged. "He's lonely, and he needs someone t take care of his daughter and keep his home runnin smoothly."

Ruth shook her head in stunned disbelief. "The boy's blind fool. He always was too inflexible and obstinate for hi own good, and that's his problem now. He's never had relationship with any woman but Alicia, so he probably feel deep down that he can't love you without being disloyal t her."

"I suppose he does," Tamara agreed, "but surely if sh loved him she wouldn't want him to spend the rest of his lif alone except for Francie."

"You're right, she wouldn't," Ruth said. "And he' know that if he'd just let himself believe it. Give him a littl time, my dear. Once you two are married and settled dow he'll come to realize that he loves you just as deeply as h loved Alicia."

"'Come to realize,'" Tamara murmured. "It sounds s upbeat and promising, like a storybook where everythin ends happily ever after. But real life doesn't always follo the guidelines. It may be that he will never let himself lov me."

Ruth looked alarmed. "If you have doubts then don't g through with this. It's never too late to back out right up t the time the final vows are said."

Tamara's eyes widened with astonishment. "Oh, I'd never do that," she said emphatically. "I love Clay. I want to marry him. It doesn't matter that he doesn't love me. I'll still be happier with him than I'd be either alone or with any other man, and I'll do all I can to make him happy, too."

Now Ruth looked as if she was going to cry. She blinked back tears and reached out to put her arms around Tamara. "You're the best thing that could have happened to my son and to Francie. She loves you wholeheartedly, and he does, too. He just hasn't let himself believe it yet."

By four o'clock, the guests had all been seated in the folding chairs that had been set up in rows in the living room. Organ music filled the air. As the soloist, a tenor from the choir of the church where the Rutledges were members, started to sing, Tamara took her place at the top of the stairs. She'd decided to make the long walk to the altar after all, but would go down the staircase since there was no aisle.

A few seconds later, Clay came out of his room and joined her. He wore a navy blue suit with a white shirt, blue tie and a single peach rose boutonniere. She'd never seen him looking more handsome as he handed her a bridal bouquet of roses that matched the wreath in her hair. He kissed her lightly on the lips. "You look like an angel," he said huskily as his gaze roamed admiringly over her. "Complete with a floral halo."

She knew she must be glowing with the happiness she felt. "And you look exactly like the groom I've always dreamed I'd have." Her voice quivered.

"I'll try hard to live up to that image," he promised.

"You already have," she said sincerely.

He put his arm around her waist, and they stood together listening to the dreamy melody and poetic lyrics of the ballad they'd chosen. Since she had no family here to give her away, she'd asked Clay if he would walk to the altar with her. He'd been inordinately pleased that she'd suggested it. "A woman shouldn't be *given* to a man in holy matrimony," he'd said. "She should come to him freely and without bonds." That's the way Tamara was coming to him, knowing the pitfalls but loving him enough to gamble her future on his kindness and consideration.

The last notes of the song died away, and after a few seconds' hesitation, the first bars of the wedding march sent shivers of exultation through Tamara.

Clay squeezed her waist, then took her hand and put it through his arm. "Here we go," he murmured, and they took the first step down the stairs to a new and promising life together.

It was after seven o'clock before the newlyweds were able to get away. The beauty of the ceremony touched Tamara more deeply than anything she'd ever experienced, and when Clay kissed his bride, it was a sweet blending of souls as well as a promise of fidelity.

Francie had looked adorable in her cream-colored ruffled dress with a peach satin sash. Her large dark eyes had sparkled with excitement as she'd watched her father and Tamara walking down the staircase toward her and Dusty, who had been Clay's best man, and she'd stood so still and reverently while the vows were taken.

Afterward, the guests lined up to be introduced to Tamara and wish the newlyweds happiness. Once that was over, dinner seemed to go on forever. Finally, however, the cake was cut, the toasts made and the bridal bouquet tossed. Tamara deliberately aimed it at Francie and was relieved when the little girl caught it. She was surprised and delighted, as Tamara had known she would be.

Now it was well after dark as they registered at the hotel in Corpus Christi where Clay had reserved the honeymoon suite. A bellhop carried their luggage and showed them to their rooms on the twentieth floor, which offered a breath taking view of the gulf. As soon as the man had shut the door behind him, Clay turned to Tamara and took her in his arms. "You look so tiny and ethereal. I'm almost afraid to touch you," he murmured softly.

She smiled against his chest. "I'm tougher than you think," she assured him, "and I like it when you touch me. I like to stroke you, too." She rubbed her palms across his shoulders and felt him tremble.

"I'll never get enough of your stroking," he said huskily and crushed her to him. "Oh, Tamara, I want you so much, need you so badly, but I don't want to hurt you...."

Her hands continued to lightly massage his back and neck as she hastened to reassure him, albeit reluctantly. She hadn't deliberately misled him, but apparently he'd misunderstood the extent of her innocence. She'd better tell him. He'd find out soon enough for himself if she didn't. "Hurt me? You won't hurt me, Clay. I'm not very experienced at lovemaking, but neither am I a virgin."

She held her breath, waiting for some sign that he was disappointed, or even angry. Instead his roaming hand found her breast and cupped it, sending tremors through her. "That's not what I meant," he said. "Certainly I don't want to hurt you physically, but I was talking about emotionally. I want you to be happy, but sometimes I'm so clumsy. Without ever meaning to, I say or do things that are insensitive—"

She leaned back in his embrace and raised her head to look at him as she broke in. "Clay, stop that. You're not clumsy and insensitive. You're sweet and considerate and I love you. I understand how you feel about me, and I accept it. So stop beating yourself—"

He lowered his head and kissed her, right on her open mouth, swallowing her words as his tongue made love to hers. "Do you understand that you are as necessary to me as the air I breathe?" he whispered in her ear. "That I'll never let you go because I couldn't live without you?"

Tamara's arms tightened around him. That sounded to her like love, but if he couldn't admit he loved her, she was willing to settle for need and want. It was all the same. He just didn't realize that yet.

"I hope you'll always believe that," she said contentedly, then sighed and shivered as his thumb and forefinger worried the hardened nub of her breast.

With his other hand, he gently pushed her into the hardness of his groin, then moaned as she slowly rubbed against him. "Sweetheart, how can I be gentle with you when you're taxing my self-control to the limit?" His fingers kneaded her buttocks.

She felt herself blush. "What makes you think I want you to be gentle?" she teased shyly. Even though her only other experience with sex had been rape, she wasn't afraid of Clay. She knew he wouldn't hurt her.

"I'm not going to ravage you," Clay said adamantly. "At least, not on our wedding night." He glanced toward the bedroom. "How about sharing a shower with me?" he murmured seductively. "That might slow us down."

Her eyes widened. "Do you really believe that?"

He shook his head and smiled. "Not for a minute."

The muscles deep in her most intimate recesses tightened. "I . . . I'd like to shower together," she said tremulously.

Without another word, he swept her up in his arms and carried her into the bathroom. As they passed through the bedroom, she noticed that the queen-size bed had already been turned down. Timidity warred with eagerness as she envisioned herself lying there with her new husband, their frenzied bodies entwined.

"Will you let me undress you?" he asked as he put her down.

She remembered the time he'd taken her clothes off before, and the thought of him doing so again was irresistible. "If you want to."

She'd changed into a flower-print dress after the reception. He found the zipper at the back of the garment and slowly lowered it. "I want to very much. I want to look at that beautiful body."

The long zipper parted, and he slipped the dress off her shoulders and let it fall to the floor. She wasn't wearing a slip and she blushed all over as she stood in front of him wearing nothing but a see-through lace teddy over her panty hose. Her first impulse was to cover herself with her hands and arms, but she conquered it and stood quietly as his gaze roamed lazily over her.

"Don't be embarrassed with me, sweetheart," he said tenderly. "I'm your husband now, and you are exquisite."

She knew by the glazed expression in his eyes that he was pleased, and she relaxed. "Can I undress you now?"

A flicker of pleasure crossed his face. "In a minute," he told her. "We're not through with you yet."

He slid the spaghetti straps off her shoulders, and the top of the garment fell to her waist. This time she did cross her arms over her bare breasts, but he smiled and unfolded them. "Don't hide yourself from me," he pleaded, and touched her with his fingertips. "So small and perfectly formed," he breathed as he leaned down and kissed each breast before taking one into his mouth. Tamara gasped and dug her fingers into his shoulders as he caressed her nipple with his tongue.

Intellectually she knew what an orgasm was. She'd read the how-to books and heard her more sophisticated friends talk, but if that was what she was working up to now, the writers and talkers hadn't even come close to describing the real thing. The excitement that was building would soon be out of control, and she wanted Clay joined with her when it happened.

It took all her willpower to push him gently away. "Please, Clay, it's...it's all happening too fast. Let me undress you...."

He smiled down at her. "Sorry, sweetheart." His voice was gravelly. "I'm being greedy. If only you weren't so tempting..." He moved back one step and grinned. "Nothing would please me more than for you to take off my clothes," he said rakishly. "Do you know where to start?"

She cocked her head and looked him over. "Not really," she drolled, "but I'll fumble around till I get it right."

"Don't fumble in the wrong places or we'll never even make it into the shower," he groaned.

"I'll be ever so careful," she promised, then immediately sent shock waves through him by tackling his belt buckle.

He uttered an urgent oath and grabbed her hands. "Not there! You start with the suit coat and work your way down and around that area."

"Oh, darn," she said mournfully, although an involuntary upward twitch at the corners of her mouth betrayed her. "And I was so looking forward to, um, soothing that swelling."

"That does it, you little tease." With a cross between a yelp and a laugh, he quickly shrugged out of his coat and began loosening his tie. "Take off the rest of your clothes and get in the shower while I undress myself, or I'll have my way with you right here on the tile floor."

"Promises, promises," she grumbled good-naturedly as she did what he told her.

The lighthearted mood was forgotten the minute he stepped, buck naked, into the shower. A prickly cascade of warm water tumbled over them, but it didn't obscure her vision. She'd never actually seen a nude man before. Certainly not her father, and she hadn't had brothers or lovers, but even without a comparison, it was obvious that her new husband was magnificent. All muscle and bone, without a bit of fat or flab.

He was studying her as intently as she was him, and she reached out and put her hands on his chest. He didn't have much chest hair, just enough to quicken her already pounding heart as she rubbed her palms over it.

He flinched when she moved them slowly down to his waist, and she noticed that his hands were clenched. He managed to stand still while she outlined his slender hips to the top of his thighs, but then he caught her by the wrists and held them. "Enough, love." His tone was thick with passion, and she realized that he was shaking. "Now it's my turn."

He picked up a bar of soap and rubbed it between his palms, then lathered her shoulders, back and arms. His hands stroking her bare skin made her shiver with need. Again he soaped his hands, then turned her so her back was against him while he caressed her breasts, lingering to brush her turgid nipples tenderly with his thumbs.

She moaned deep in her throat. It felt so good. He knew just how and where to touch her to make her writhe with need.

Then he moved downward to her stomach, and her muscles jumped and twisted into knots beneath his talented hands. He caught his breath and ground his hardness into the soft rise of her buttocks. His hand found its target and sent shock waves of pleasure to the very core of her being as his fingers gently probed. The intensity of it frightened her, and she gasped and cried out, "Clay, don't. Not yet. Not without you."

His fingers stilled, but he continued to cradle her. "It's all right, sweetheart." His tone was hoarse with strain, but even so, he sounded inordinately pleased. "This is just the beginning. It gets better, and I promise I'll be right with you."

She was certain he didn't understand the intensity of the feelings he was stirring in her. Surely it couldn't get any better. Catching his hand in hers, she turned in his embrace and looked up at him. "Can we go to bed now?" she asked tremulously.

He crushed her to him and rubbed his cheek in her slick, wet hair as the pulsating water continued to spray over them. "We'll do whatever you want to do," he assured her and covered her mouth with his, which escalated the shock waves and made her forget her caution and whimper for more.

A moment later, he released her and turned off the shower. After he'd helped her out of the stall and rubbed her down briskly with one of the big white bath towels, he handed her a smaller one for her hair while he dried himself off.

Tamara had been raised to think of the body as something to be covered at all times, and she felt guilty watching Clay wandering around nude with such unselfconscious grace. Still, she couldn't keep her eyes off him. He was a study in symmetry, like a Rodin sculpture come to life.

She hoped that soon she could feel as free and easy with him as he seemed to be with her. She didn't want a wall of false modesty between them. She didn't want *anything* between them, not even clothes.

He glanced up, caught her looking at him and winked. She felt the heat of the color that suffused her face and hated it, but he smiled, threw down his towel and reached for her. "You'll get used to seeing a man in your bedroom without any clothes on," he promised her. "You're bound to, because it's going to be a nightly occurrence."

"Oh, I hope it is," she said just before he again swept her into his arms. Flicking off the bathroom light, he carried her to the waiting bed.

"Would you be more comfortable with the light off?" he asked solicitously.

She nodded. "Do you mind?"

He leaned down and kissed her as he turned off the bedside lamp. "Not a bit. We have the rest of our lives to get to know each other. This is just the beginning."

He walked over to the window and pulled open the heavy drape that covered it. The full moon shot a moonbeam into the room and silhouetted Clay as he moved toward the bed.

He climbed in beside Tamara and took her in his arms, and after that she was unaware of anything but the enchantment he wove around and through her with his seeking mouth and gentle but insistently probing hands.

He brought her to the brink of frenzy, then joined his body with hers for the explosion that sent her soaring past rapture to ecstasy, and beyond to a total oneness with this man who was now and forever her love, her life, her husband.

Chapter Nine

It was hot that summer in San Antonio and the air was saturated and steamy with moisture. Residents and tourists alike holed up in their air-conditioned abodes or scurried to department stores and theaters in search of relief.

Not that Tamara Houston Rutledge noticed. She was much too ecstatic to let a little thing like scorching heat annoy her. In fact, nothing ruffled her composure. How could it? She had everything she needed to keep her happy and content—her beloved daughter and a husband that most women only dreamed about.

After that glorious honeymoon spent mostly in bed, they'd come home to happiness unbounded. If she'd ever had doubts about marrying a man who professed not to love her, they were gone. Clay was the perfect husband and lover. Attentive, solicitous and caring. It's true that even in their most intimate moments he never said "I love you," but a lot of wives complained that their husbands never actually told them that in so many words.

With Clay it wasn't necessary. He showed his devotion to her in the way he treated her. The day after she'd agreed to marry him, he'd quietly removed Alicia's portrait from the library wall and put it in storage. He'd even arranged to have the master bedroom completely redecorated and refurnished while they were in Corpus Christi, so that when she came back into his home as his wife, all traces of Alicia had been removed.

Several postnuptial parties had been given for Tamara and Clay by neighbors, friends and business acquaintances, and even though all of them had been friends of Alicia's, they'd welcomed Tamara and seemed genuinely happy that Clay had married again.

But most rewarding of all was Francie's unconditional acceptance of Tamara as her father's wife and her mother. Although Clay wouldn't allow Francie to call her Mother or any other variation of that title, it was a minor disappointment compared to the joy of sharing such a close and necessary part of her daughter's life.

The summer had flown by, and by the third Saturday in October Tamara and Clay had been married three months. Francie had turned eight in August and had gone into third grade at The Mission Trail Academy. Tamara had had the privilege and the thrill of celebrating the birthday with her. She'd missed all the others, but never again would she let that happen.

It was early afternoon. Francie had gone to a party for one of her little friends in the neighborhood, Clay was in his study at the back of the house, and Tamara was baking cookies in the kitchen. She loved cooking for her family. Her family. What a beautiful ring those two words used together had. She was truly blessed.

Clay sat at his desk and tried to concentrate on the figures in the bank statement he held in his hand. However, the image of Tamara bustling around the kitchen in tight red jeans that outlined her cute little round behind and slender legs kept distracting him. His house was a totally different place since she'd come to him, first as Francie's nanny, then as his wife.

He chuckled and shifted in his chair as he realized that his jeans were tight, too, but for a more compelling reason. He'd been insatiably addicted to her ever since the first night of their honeymoon, and the urge to whisk her out of the kitchen and up to the bedroom right now was almost overwhelming.

With some effort, he resisted, afraid that if he didn't practice a little restraint she'd think that was all he wanted her for. Nothing could be further from the truth, although before they were married he'd tried to tell himself otherwise.

He was still confused about his feelings. How could he care so intensely for her when Alicia had been his love, his life? There were periods when days went by without him thinking of his late wife. Even the term "late wife" didn't apply anymore, because Tamara was now his wife and she was very much alive. Thank God for that, but his emotions didn't make sense, and it bothered him.

The aroma of freshly baked peanut butter cookies and the sound of Tamara singing while she worked wrested his confused thinking back to a more even keel. She had a nice singing voice, sweet and about midrange. When he'd first commented on it, she'd told him she'd sung in school and church choirs when she was growing up. That would account for the trained timbre of her tone.

It was evident that she'd had a quality upbringing, but she never talked about her parents or her childhood. All he knew was that she and her parents were estranged, but what she meant by that he had no idea. Had there been a slight misunderstanding, or did they hate each other?

He couldn't imagine Tamara hating anyone, and he sure couldn't imagine anyone hating her. She was much too lov ing for that. On the other hand, what did he really know about her? Every time he'd tried to question her about her background, she'd changed the subject, usually so subtly that he hadn't even realized she'd done it.

Well, it was really none of his business. When she wanted to tell him about it, she would. Until then, he wasn't going to pry.

This time it was the phone that shook him out of his reverie, and since it was right there on the desk, he caught it on the first ring. "Rutledge residence, Clay speaking."

"Clay, this is Victor York."

Clay was surprised. Victor York was his lawyer, but theirs was strictly a business relationship. They never called each other at home. "Vic, how are you? It's been awhile, man."

"Yeah, it has. How's everything with you? I heard you recently got married."

Clay blinked. Was Vic calling just to congratulate him? "Yes, I did. We're very happy."

"Glad to hear it. Couldn't have happened to a nicer guy."

There was an awkward silence before Victor spoke again. He sounded reluctant. "Look, Clay, I don't want to upset you, but I just had a call from Ms. Underwood, the manager of that home for pregnant girls in Fort Worth where your adopted child was born."

A worm of fear curled in Clay's gut. "Yes, I remember. What does this have to do with me?"

"Probably nothing important, but she tells me that they recently found the file on your child's birth mother in the drawer of an employee's desk, although it had been sealed away in the closed files years ago."

The fear grew and clawed at Clay. "For God's sake, get to the point, Vic."

"The point is that they investigated, and the employee, a temporary who was filling in for a caseworker on extended sick leave, admitted he'd accepted a bribe for information about your little girl."

Clay swore, loudly and lustily, as anger sent his blood rushing through his veins. "If this causes a problem with Francie, I'll kill that son of a bitch and sue the hell out of the maternity home—"

"Now hold on," Vic yelled above the clamor Clay was making. "Don't go off half-cocked. The home has it under control. The employee has been fired and subject to a huge fine, plus he's 'singing like a bird' as they used to say in old gangster movies."

Clay got to his feet. "This is not funny, Vic," he growled.

On the other end of the line, the attorney sighed. "I know that, Clay, but it's not necessarily a tragedy, either. A private detective in Ames, Iowa has also been arrested. He's the one who contacted the home and bribed the man way back in June."

Ames, Iowa? That's where Tamara used to live. What an odd coincidence. "What did he want to know, and what was he going to do with the information?"

"Well...he wanted to know who had adopted Tamara Houston's baby...."

The explosion that rocked through Clay nearly toppled him. He grabbed the back of the chair and plopped down into it as his legs gave way.

Tamara Houston! No! It was just a diabolical coincidence. It couldn't be his Tamara. She'd never been married before. Never had a child. His mind was playing tricks on him.

Vic was hollering into the phone. "Clay? Clay, are you still there? Are you listening?"

Clay tried to speak but his throat was so dry and parched that nothing came out. He cleared it and tried again. This time his voice worked, but it was rusty. "Ta-Tamara Hou-Houston?"

"Yeah, that's the name of the birth mother of your little girl. They gave me her name and last known address since she'd already breached the confidentiality of the case. At the time her baby was born she was seventeen years old and lived in a little backwater town in Iowa with her parents. As of June of this year, she was living in Ames. That's when she hired the private detective.''

Clay's breath was coming in gasps, and he felt light-headed. "She—she hired the investigator?"

"That's what I said. Clay, are you all right?" he asked anxiously.

Clay made a massive effort to pull himself together. He couldn't let Vic know just how brutally shocked he really was. "No, I'm not all right," he admitted. "I'm mad as hell. No one is going to take my daughter away from me! No one!"

"No one's trying to," Vic countered sharply. "Dammit all, Clay, pay attention to what I'm trying to tell you. This woman, Tamara Houston, walked into the P.I.'s office one day and said she'd given up a baby girl for adoption when she was a teenager, and she wanted him to find out who had adopted her. At first the guy refused, said he didn't believe in women trying to reclaim a child they'd given up years before."

A wave of nausea hit Clay in the stomach. "But she talked him into doing it anyway," he said bitterly, knowing only too well the effect Tamara Houston could have on a man.

"I guess you could say that. She assured him that she had no intention of claiming the child. She just wanted to know where she was and if she was happy and well treated."

"How touching," Clay muttered sarcastically. "So how come it took her almost eight years? The kid could have been maimed for life or killed by unfit adoptive parents in that time."

"Clay, I know this has been a shock, but you can't have it both ways. Are you mad because she tried to find her child or because it took her so long to decide she wanted to?"

"Victor, you have no conception of the extent of my rage." His tone was hard and cold. "I can be mad at her for things you haven't even thought of yet. I'll deal with her. You press charges against that P.I. Get his license revoked, and see to it that he never gets another one, anywhere.''

Tamara took the last pan of cookies out of the oven and turned it off. Mingled aromas of peanut butter and chocolate from the two different batches she'd made drifted tantalizingly in the air. As soon as she cleaned up the kitchen, she'd take a plate of them to Clay, although she was surprised he hadn't smelled them and come to sample a few before this.

She was stacking dirty dishes in the dishwasher when she heard a thundering boom from the direction of the study, like something heavy being thrown against the wall. She jumped and turned off the water. Good heavens, what was that!

"Clay!" she called as she hurried toward the noise, but her cry was drowned out by another deafening crash that sounded as if everything breakable in the room had been dropped and splintered.

"Darling, what's happened?" she cried again and broke into a run. The door to the study was closed so she grabbed the knob and twisted. It wouldn't turn. The door was locked!

"Clay, what's going on?" she shouted as she frantically rattled the knob. "The door's locked. Let me in!"

She heard a muffled oath before he bellowed, "Go away.''

Go away? What kind of a response was that? Why had he locked her out, and what was he doing?

This time she pounded on the door as her fear blended with anger. "Clay Rutledge, let me in! What happened? Did something fall? Are you hurt?''

"Nothing fell and I'm not hurt." His tone was grim. "Just leave me the hell alone!''

For the first time she realized that he was mad. No, not just mad, furious. And with her! But what had she done?

Now Tamara was really scared. She'd never known Clay to be so angry before, and there certainly hadn't been anything wrong when they woke up that morning. They'd spent an hour making love before they heard Francie getting up.

He'd been happy and cheerful right through lunch and up to the time he'd gone to his study where he always worked on personal and family business accounts.

He'd said he was going to check his bank statements. Had he found something in them that had upset him so? That hardly seemed likely. Nothing short of total financial collapse could bring on a reaction like this.

Frantically she pounded on the door again. "Clay, stop this nonsense. Unlock the door and let me in. Please. I'm worried."

There was no answer, and she realized that her legs were shaking. With weary resignation she sat down on the floor directly across from the study door, with her back against the wall and her knees drawn up under her chin. It wasn't like Clay to deliberately upset her, and she wasn't going to let him out of her sight until he told her what was the matter.

A few minutes later the door opened and he stood before her, weaving slightly as though recovering from a blow. She gasped and got to her feet. "Darling, what happened?" She started to reach out to him, but to her amazement he took a step backward.

"Don't touch me!" His tone was low, but harsh and devoid of emotion, and his face was white and drawn. However it was the look in his eyes that stunned her. They had darkened to almost black, and were blazing.

Tamara didn't even try to conceal her hurt. She wasn't going to stand there passively and let him abuse her with words, but on the other hand, there could no longer be any doubt about why he was upset. He was angry with *her*. No, more than angry. He was furious!

Ever the optimist, she was sure that whatever had enraged him could be sorted out if they could just talk calmly, like the two rational people they were. She swallowed and lowered her arms to her sides. "Clay, I won't be treated like this. I'm your wife. I'm entitled to know what's happened to make you lash out at me this way."

He glared at her. "Oh, really. Entitled, are you? So how come you're the only privileged one in this family? Don't you think I was entitled to know before I invited you into my home and my life that you're the birth mother of my adopted daughter?"

It was as if he'd thrown a bucket of ice water over her. The shock sent her body into a spasm. She staggered back against the wall and stared at him. "How did you—" She clamped her mouth shut, but the murderous look on his face told her the damage was already done.

"How did I find out?" His tone was glacial. "Well, you sure as hell didn't tell me."

"Clay, I—"

"Did you honestly think you could get away with bribery and lies?" he interrupted as if she hadn't spoken.

She blinked. "Bribery?"

"Tell me, what was your original plan? Did you come down here to take Francie away from me and then decide, when you found out I was a widower, that seducing me into marrying you was an easier way to get her? Or did you come knowing I was single and wouldn't be able to resist your bewitching deception?"

"Clay, please. You don't understand—"

"You're right. I don't. I don't understand how any woman, any *mother*, could give her baby away and then, years later, after the child is part of a loving family, track it down and selfishly disrupt its whole life—"

"I didn't! Dammit, Clay, listen to me—"

"Listen to you?" He spit out the words as though they had a bad taste, but then he paused. "All right, I'll listen.

Just answer two questions. One, are you Francie's birth mother?''

Tamara wanted no more lies between them, and answered honestly. "Yes, I am."

Clay showed no emotion. "Two, did you know I was her adoptive father when you came to my office that first day?"

Tamara saw the trap now, but it was too late to avoid it. She looked away from him. "Yes, I did, but—"

"So even the toothache was a lie, and still you expect me to listen to you? Are you perhaps thinking of blackmailing me? Offering not to try to regain custody if I'll pay you?"

Tamara gasped. "That's a rotten thing to say."

"Oh, that's mild compared to the things I've been thinking but haven't said," he declared coldly. "I've been hearing your siren song and been mesmerized by it for months. I'm sure as hell not going to give you a chance to weave another spell."

He turned abruptly and strode down the hall toward the entryway. "Where are you going?" Tamara called.

"Out," he answered as he opened the door. He slammed it shut behind him.

The fierce bang of the door seemed to sever the invisible cord of determination that held her upright, and she slowly slumped to the floor. Too traumatized even to cry, she lay on the thick carpet where she'd fallen, her face cradled in her folded arms, until she heard the grandfather clock in the living room chime the hour of four.

It was time to pick up Francie from the party and bring her home.

Slowly she pushed herself to a sitting position. Her head swam, but she managed to stand and walk into the bathroom. At first she didn't recognize the reflection in the mirror. She looked almost as bad as Clay had. Her face was white and pinched, her hair disheveled, and her eyes stared back at her from a sunken depth of misery.

She couldn't let Francie and her little friends see her looking like this, but neither did she have time for a shower and a complete makeup job. Instead she splashed cold water on her face, then slapped at her cheeks in an effort to put some color back into them. A touch of lipstick and blusher and a brisk brushing of her hair made her a little more presentable, and with the addition of dark glasses, she rushed out of the house.

Clay's car wasn't in the garage, but the little red Jaguar he'd bought her as a wedding present was. She got in and drove the few blocks to the birthday girl's house.

The door chime was answered by the girl's mother, who looked at Tamara with surprise. "Hi, Tamara," she said as she stepped back. "Come on in. What can I do for you?"

Tamara started to enter, then stopped, bewildered by the question. "I came for Francie, Maybelle. You did say four o'clock, didn't you? Sorry I'm a little late—"

"But Francie's not here," Maybelle said. "Clay picked her up about an hour ago. He said something had come up and he was taking her to see her grandparents." Tamara had run through a gauntlet of emotions in the past few hours, but now it was fear that gripped her. It must have shown because Maybelle looked concerned. "It was all right to let her go with him, wasn't it? I mean, he is her father."

Tamara swallowed. "Yes. Yes, of course. I guess Clay and I just got our signals crossed. Sorry I bothered you."

They said their goodbyes and Tamara hurried back to the car, then sat there and shook. Why had Clay gone to the ranch and taken Francie with him? Why hadn't he told her that's what he was going to do? When would they be back?

When she was reasonably sure she could drive the car without causing an accident, she started the engine and went back to the house and took up her vigil.

For the first couple of hours she managed to keep busy enough to be able to push her fears to the back of her mind. Clay was mad at her, and he'd wanted to put some distance between them, so he'd taken Francie and driven to the ranch. They'd be back when he'd cooled off a little.

From seven to nine she tried to watch television, but every time she heard a car go by, she jumped up and looked out the window to see if it was them. It never was.

From nine to ten she paced from one window to another, hoping to catch a glimpse of his car lights coming down the street.

At five past ten she dialed the number at the ranch. When she heard the phone ring at the other end, she shivered with fear. What if they weren't there? What if Clay had just told Maybelle that's where they were going because he didn't want Tamara to know where they were? My God, would he abduct his own daughter to keep her away from her natural mother?

Eventually the phone was answered by Ruth.

"Ruth, this is Tamara. Are...are Clay and Francie there?" She held her breath waiting for an answer.

When it came, it was neither friendly nor unfriendly, but neutral. "Yes, they are, Tamara. Didn't you know that?"

"N-not for sure," she stammered. "May I speak to Clay?"

"I'll get him," Ruth said, and then Tamara listened to a babble of voices too far away to be able to distinguish what was being said.

Finally Ruth returned. "I'm sorry, Tamara, but Clay says he won't talk to you." A whimper broke through Tamara's precarious control, followed by a sob. "Tamara, are you all right?" Ruth asked anxiously. "What on earth is going on? Clay came out here looking and sounding like a wild man. He says you're trying to take Francie away from him."

For the first time since all this started, tears filled Tamara's eyes and spilled down her cheeks. "That's not true," she cried. "That was never my intent."

"But you are the child's natural mother?"

Tamara grabbed a tissue from the box by the phone and blew her nose. "Yes, but I don't know how he found out...."

She knew immediately that that was the wrong thing to say.

"I don't suppose it ever occurred to you to tell him yourself?" The neutrality in Ruth's tone had just tottered, and not in Tamara's favor.

"Oh, Ruth, I've agonized over that right from the start." Tamara mopped at the tears but couldn't stop the flow. "Obviously I made the wrong decision, but I never meant him any harm."

"But you did harm him," Ruth said, her anger evident now. "Viciously and without mercy. He's been here for hours and he still hasn't calmed down enough to give us a coherent account of what's happened. I'm going to find that hard to forgive, and I doubt that he ever will."

A series of sobs shook Tamara, and it was a moment before she could speak. "But you haven't even heard my side of the story. Nobody has."

"That's true," Ruth admitted. "But I've seen what you did to my son, and frankly I don't know how there could possibly be any excuse for it."

Tamara knew her mother-in-law had a right to be outraged. She'd feel the same if anyone hurt Francie the way she'd wounded Clay. For that matter, she'd never forgive herself for the anguish she'd caused her husband. He'd opened his heart as well as his home to her, and she'd repaid him with lies and deceit.

She took another tissue and blew her nose again. "Ruth is...is Francie all right? Is she frightened or upset?"

"Francie's fine. As soon as we realized how devastated Clay was, Jim took her to his house. Kathy's looking after her."

Tamara felt a wave of relief. At least her daughter wasn't in the middle of this dreadful scene. She'd do whatever it took to keep it that way. On the other hand, she'd obviously lost the approval of the Rutledge clan. "I ... I guess the whole family is there and aware of what's happened?"

She hadn't meant it to be a question, but it came out that way. "Yes, of course they are. That's what families are for. To support each other in times of crisis."

"I wouldn't know," Tamara mused aloud. "I never had a family who did that for me." She hadn't meant to speak her thoughts, and quickly changed the subject. The last thing she wanted was to come across as a sniveling, poor-little-me victim. "Are ... that is ... will Clay and Francie be coming home tonight?"

There was silence for a moment before Ruth answered, "I doubt it, but I'll ask him if you want me to."

Tamara already knew the answer, but she'd had to ask just in case there was reason to hope. "No, don't bother him."

Another series of sobs made talking impossible and she hung up the phone and let the persistent tears flow freely to batter her already tattered control.

Chapter Ten

Tamara awoke the following morning, Sunday, alone. In the bed and in the house. Clay hadn't come back, and she had no idea when he would. This was the first night they'd spent apart since their wedding, and she was heartbroken and lost.

Last night she'd fallen asleep almost as soon as she'd crawled between the sheets, exhausted both emotionally and physically after the battering her psyche had taken. But it was a troubled sleep peopled with lost children and accusing loved ones, faceless but familiar, who pointed their fingers at her in gestures of shame and disappointment.

After dragging herself out of bed, she headed for the bathroom and stood under a hot, stinging shower. When at last she turned off the water, her skin was blotched red and the room was filled with steam, but she did feel partially reinvigorated.

When she'd finished dressing in white jeans and a black-and-white-checked shirt she went downstairs to the kitchen and made coffee. She hadn't had anything to eat since lunch the day before, but the thought of food turned her stomach.

While she was waiting for the coffee to perk, she was startled to hear a key being inserted in the front door. Her heart pounded. It was Clay. It had to be. The two of them were the only ones who had keys to the house.

The door opened, then closed, and she dropped the mug she'd just taken from the cupboard. It landed on the tile counter and broke into pieces, but she hardly noticed as she hurried toward the entryway.

Clay was leaning against the door just staring into space. She reached out her arms. "Darling, please forgive me. I'm so sorry..." Her words trailed off, stopped by the look he turned on her before she got close enough to touch him. It was hostile and stony.

If she'd seen him on the street, she wouldn't have known him. His black hair, usually so immaculately groomed, was tousled and uncombed. His eyes had tiny red veins and were sunken and ringed with dark shadows, and a day's prickly growth of black beard was evidence that he hadn't shaved yet this morning.

He didn't say anything, just remained there glaring at her, totally unapproachable. She felt sick. Obviously he hadn't returned to effect a reconciliation. It was then that she realized she hadn't seen or heard Francie and blurted, "Where's Francie?"

He straightened, and his jaw clenched even tighter. "Don't worry. I've taken care of her all her life. I'm not about to botch the job now. She's staying at the ranch with Mom and Dad until you and I get things settled between us."

Tamara shook her head remorsefully. She hated causing this good, gentle man so much grief, but every time she opened her mouth to speak she only added to it. "Clay, *you* are my first concern, my only one right now, because I know you wouldn't let anything happen to Francie, but I'd expected her to be with you.''

For a moment he seemed to totter, but then he regained his balance. ''Don't lie to me anymore, Tamara. I can't take it,'' he said wearily. He looked so...so alone and defeated that it was all she could do not to close the distance between them and take him in her arms, but his whole countenance warned her to stay away and not invade his space.

''I'm not lying to you, love,'' she said instead. ''I've never lied about my feelings for you. Look, I've just made coffee. Come into the kitchen and have a cup. Have you eaten?''

His only reaction was to shake his head.

''Then I'll fix breakfast.'' She turned and walked slowly toward the kitchen, not knowing if he would follow her or not.

''I don't want to eat,'' he said.

She managed to keep her voice calm as she spoke over her shoulder. ''I'll just fix some tea and toast.''

She was relieved to hear him following behind her, and began preparing the snack while he pulled a chair away from the table and almost fell into it. Tamara very much doubted that he'd even been to bed last night, let alone slept. He was in a deep state of shock, but she knew he wasn't going to let her help him. She'd have to be careful not to drive him away again. It was a miracle he'd arrived at the house all in one piece. It could have been disastrous for him to handle a car in his present condition.

It only took a few minutes to heat water for tea in the microwave and brown two slices of bread in the toaster. ''Here, you have to eat something,'' she told him as she set the plate and cup before him.

He nodded and dutifully took a bite but didn't invite her to sit with him. Not that she'd ordinarily need an invitation, but now she wasn't going to assume anything where he was concerned. Instead she left the kitchen and went outside to get the newspaper. Her next-door neighbor, the wife of a dermatologist and an avid gardener, was pruning the stately row of tree roses between their two houses and started a conversation, which Tamara couldn't terminate quickly without being rude.

It was five minutes or more before she could break away, and when she got back to the kitchen, she found Clay asleep with his head resting on his arms. Her heart brimmed with compassion. Poor darling. He was totally wiped out.

After quietly stacking the empty dishes, she put them in the sink, then moved to stand over him and watch while he slept. He looked so uncomfortable and so vulnerable, slumped over on the table that way. If only he'd let her tell him her side of the story, he might not feel so betrayed.

She leaned over and put her arms around him, then nuzzled his stubbly cheek and the side of his throat. She knew it was unfair of her to take advantage of him when he was in no condition to fend her off, but he wouldn't let her near him when he was awake.

Maybe subliminally he'd be aware of her touch and be comforted by it. Then again, maybe he'd be even angrier with her for breaching his privacy.

He began to stir and she shook him gently. "Clay, wake up and let me help you upstairs to bed where you'll be more comfortable." Her voice was husky with emotion.

He raised his head. "Dammit, Tamara, don't take care of me," he muttered gruffly, putting his head back down. "I don't need a mother. I already have one."

She was relieved that at least he hadn't fought her off. She still had her arms around him as she leaned over again and spoke against his ear. "I know, sweetheart, but you need rest, and the best place to get that is in bed. Just wake up long enough for me to get you upstairs—"

This time he not only raised his head, but he also shook her away from him and sat up. "I don't need help," he grated and got unsteadily to his feet, then promptly disproved the statement by swaying dangerously.

He reached out and clutched her to steady himself. She balanced firmly on her feet and put her arms around his waist. For a moment they just stood there hugging each other. Tamara could feel his heart pounding against her as his embrace gentled from a grab to a caress. Her own heart was racing, and her legs turned to mush. She melted into him and he cradled her there.

But only for a moment. Then he pushed her away and muttered an expletive as he turned and walked to the staircase. She was right behind him as he pulled himself up by the railing one step at a time.

He stumbled into the master bedroom and dropped down to sit on the side of the bed. He tried to lift one foot to untie his shoe, but couldn't quite make it. Tamara knelt in front of him. "Let me do it," she said and untied the shoe and slipped it off his foot.

"I can undress myself," he protested, but didn't object when she removed the other one, as well.

When she'd finished, he rolled over and stretched out on the roomy bed with a groan. He was lying on the spread, but she wasn't going to make him get up again. Instead she unbuttoned his shirt to the middle of his chest, then unsnapped the waistband of his jeans so he could rest more comfortably. From the linen closet in the hallway, she pulled out a lightweight blanket and covered him.

By this time he was asleep, or at least she thought he was, so she gave in to the overpowering temptation to kiss him good-night. She leaned down to stroke a lock of hair back off his forehead and press her eager mouth against his.

To her great surprise, his hands clamped around her arms and he kissed her back, hard and lustily. "Oh, darling, I love you so much," he whispered. Then his hands dropped away and he immediately fell into a deep slumber.

Tamara's feet floated six inches off the ground as she softly closed the bedroom door and drifted downstairs.

I love you so much. I love you so much. He'd admitted it. He'd actually said it to her. *I love you.*

Did that mean he was going to forgive her? That he still wanted her even though she'd deceived him? That he'd acknowledge her as Francie's real mother? That he was willing to give her babies that were his and hers together?

Her euphoria lasted approximately fifteen minutes, until she'd calmed down enough to let go of the beautiful fantasy and allow a chunk of reality to drop into the dream.

She first tripped over the actuality of the situation when she started making plans for dinner. She was standing in front of the open door to the freezer surveying their meat supply. Let's see, Clay likes barbecued ribs, but Francie doesn't care for them. On the other hand, Francie and Clay both liked chicken—

Then it hit her. Francie wasn't here. Clay had left her at the ranch with his parents. But why had he done that if he'd come home this morning to tell Tamara he loved her and all was forgiven? And why was he still so deeply anguished if he'd resolved the problem to his satisfaction? Why was he still so furious with her if he'd suddenly discovered that she was the love of his life and he couldn't live without her?

It was then that the fantasy shattered completely and the cold, hard truth confronted her. *Clay's not in love with you, you dimwit! He doesn't even like you. In fact, he can barely stand to be around you. Sure he said "I love you" but he wasn't talking to you. In that netherworld between total exhaustion and sleep he thought it was Alicia who was kissing him. It's Alicia he wants. Alicia he still loves so desperately that he'll even conjure up her ghost rather than accept you as a substitute.*

Listlessly she shut the freezer door and turned away.

After cleaning up the shards of the mug on the counter, she went into the library and picked up the phone to dial the ranch. Clay's mother answered.

"Ruth, this is Tamara," she said, and even she could hear the agony in her tone. "I just want to let you know that Clay is here. He's still furious with me, but I managed to get him to eat a little before he fell asleep at the table. I put him to bed and he's resting comfortably. He'll probably sleep for hours."

"I appreciate your calling to tell me that, Tamara," Ruth said gratefully. "I was so worried when he took off in the car. You say you put him to bed?"

Tamara caught the implication. "Don't read anything into that," she warned. "He only barely tolerated my help, and then only because he'd never have made it on his own. I...I guess you could say he's in a state of collapse, and I don't know what to do." She didn't even try to disguise her fear. "I know he won't let me take him to the doctor...." She finished on a sob.

"If you're asking my advice, I suggest that you do nothing," Ruth said. "Just let him sleep. He needs that more than anything. It's been my experience in raising a family that there's a lot of healing power in deep, sound slumber." She hesitated, then spoke again. "Now let's talk about you. You sound as upset as Clay. Are you all right?"

Tamara choked back another sob. She wasn't going to cry anymore. She had no tears left, and the dry sobs made her ill. "I feel like I've been poleaxed," she said truthfully, "but I'm a survivor. I've had plenty of practice, so I suppose I'll survive this time, too. If I could only make Clay listen to my side of this debacle, but he's so mad at me—"

"He's hurting badly, and he's pretty much unstrung right now," Ruth interrupted. "Fortunately he's not a drinker, but you'll have to give him time to pull himself together. Meanwhile, if you want to talk, I'm willing to listen."

Tamara's eyes widened. "You are?"

"Of course." Ruth sounded as if she really meant it. "I'm sorry I was angry with you on the phone yesterday, but Clay was talking like a madman and making no sense at all. The whole family was in an uproar. If you can start at the beginning and tell me exactly what's happened, I'd be ever so grateful."

Tamara felt light-headed. She was finally going to get a chance to tell her side. Ruth might not believe her, but at least she'd listen and maybe try to understand. "I...I can tell you what led to the blowup yesterday, but I still don't know what happened just before Clay came storming out of the study."

She began with her family background, then the rape, her pregnancy and her parents' unyielding opposition to her keeping her baby. She told of her heartbreak when she signed the child over for adoption, her estrangement from her parents and, finally, her decision to try to find her daughter.

"I never, ever, intended to interfere in Francie's life," she said raggedly. "All I wanted was to see her and make sure she was well cared for. When I came to San Antonio, I had no idea Clay's wife had died. Then, when I found out he was a widower and needed a nanny for Francie...well, surely you can understand... It was much too tempting a situation to ignore."

Another sob nearly shook her, and she took a deep breath. "I should have told Clay I was Francie's birth mother, but I knew he'd send me away and I just couldn't do it. I love him as much as I love her, and I would never harm either of them."

There was silence on both ends of the line, then Ruth spoke. "Do you swear you'll never try to take Francie away from Clay?"

"I swear, as God is my witness," Tamara said fervently. "Clay is her father, both legally and spiritually, and Alicia was her mother. That's a bond I couldn't break even if I wanted to. Francie likes me, but she adores her father and the memory of her mother. She'll never know of my relationship to her unless Clay tells her.''

Again there was a short period of silence before Ruth spoke. ''I want to believe you, Tamara. Actually, I do believe you, but you understand that my first loyalty is to my son.''

''That's as it should be,'' Tamara hastened to assure her. ''I only wish my mother had been more like you. Would it be possible . . . ? That is, could I speak to Francie? I promise not to upset her.''

This time the silence at the other end of the line was longer, and Tamara wasn't surprised when Ruth finally said, ''I'm sorry, but Clayton left explicit instructions that you were not to speak to Francie on the phone or be allowed to see her. The ranch hands have orders not to let you on the property.''

A cold wave of hopelessness swept through Tamara, and now she was the one who couldn't speak. Although Clay had never touched her in anger, she felt battered and bruised. What had she done that was so unspeakably wrong? She'd lied to him, yes, but never with the intent to hurt or destroy. She'd given him her love without condition or reserve, and he'd accepted it, thrived on it, even though he admitted that he couldn't return it. So why was he so unyielding, so quick to think the worst of her?

When she finally found her voice, it was raw with pain. ''I understand. Thank you for listening to my explanation—''

Her voice broke and she severed the connection.

Clay slept until midafternoon. Tamara filled the empty hours with meaningless activity. She tried reading. First the newspaper, then a magazine that came in the morning mail and finally a novel the critics raved about, but she retained nothing. Her mind was like an open-ended vacuum that sucked the words in and immediately blew them out without processing them.

When she began to feel light-headed, she realized it was from not having eaten for so long. She heated a can of soup and forced herself to swallow it, then turned on the television. The noon news was mildly interesting, but everything after that was so dull that she finally turned the set off and curled up on the sofa. Her eyes burned from tears, both those shed and those held back. Maybe if she rested them for a while...

Tamara stirred uneasily and burrowed more comfortably into the cushions. There was something amiss. She felt a crawly sensation at the back of her neck, as if she was being watched, but she couldn't wake up. Besides, she was alone in the house, except for—

Her eyes flew open, and she saw Clay standing beside the sofa looking down at her. He'd showered, shaved and changed clothes, and looked not only more rested, but more alert and able to function. There was also the oddest expression on his face, almost like a mixture of compassion and regret. But before she could decipher it, it was gone, replaced by a frown.

She pushed herself up and rubbed at her eyes. "I didn't hear you. Guess I dozed off...."

"You put me to bed this morning," he said, his tone devoid of emotion. "Why didn't you go to bed, too, instead of trying to sleep on that uncomfortable sofa?"

She blinked, confused. "I didn't think you'd want me to sleep with you."

He winced. "Oh, for God's sake, Tamara, there are enough bedrooms in this house to qualify it as a hotel. You could have slept in one of those."

Obviously she'd said the wrong thing again. Why was it that these past two days she hadn't been able to open her mouth without saying something stupid? You'd think she was a bubblehead instead of a college graduate. She was going to have to start thinking before she spoke.

Deciding that a change of subject was imperative, she stood and moved toward the hall. "I think we both need to eat," she said, walking toward the kitchen while he took matching strides beside her. "Are you up to a full meal, or would you prefer something lighter?" She was desperately trying to steer the conversation away from their problem until they'd had some nourishment, but he caught her by the arms and turned her toward him.

"I'll tell you what I'm not up to," he said, and there was resignation in his tone, "and that's fighting with you. It tears me apart, so let's stop sparring with each other and try to come to some kind of settlement."

She looked up at him and knew that the terror wrought by that word must show in her eyes. "A . . . a settlement?"

He looked puzzled. "Of course. Hell, Tamara, I have a right to know what you thought you were going to accomplish with this grand scheme of yours. Did you have this whole thing, including marriage to me, planned before you came down here, or did you wing it once you got here?"

It appeared that he wasn't going to give her the benefit of the doubt, but he may have meant "settlement" as in "find out what happened," rather than as in "alimony." *Oh, please, God, let that be the case.*

"I came here for just one reason," she said, "and that was to see my daughter and make sure she was happy and healthy. I had no intention of making myself known to any of you. I only found out you were a widower after I arrived here. If you hadn't mentioned that you needed a house-keeper that day in your office, I'd have left the following morning to go back home." She ran her fingers through her hair and brushed it back. "Give me a little credit, Clay. I had no way of knowing I was going to fall in love with you!"

He actually cringed at her outburst and turned away. 'Don't say that," he demanded hoarsely. "I don't want to hear any more of your lies. All I want from you now is the truth."

Tamara slumped against the wall. Now that Clay was ready to listen to her explanation she wasn't sure that she was up to giving it to him. He was too suspicious and bitter. They would probably just tear each other apart.

"That's what I'm going to tell you," she said. "The whole truth and nothing but. First, though, I'll fix us something to eat. It takes a lot of energy to quarrel with someone you love, and we've both nearly depleted ours. Is a dish of ice cream okay?"

He nodded without turning to look at her. "I'll wait in the library," he said and walked away.

Tamara joined him a few minutes later carrying a tray with large bowls of cherry vanilla ice cream and tall glasses of iced tea. She put it on the coffee table, then handed one of the bowls to Clay, who was sitting in his leather chair by the fireplace, and put his glass on the lamp table beside him.

She seated herself on the sofa and picked up her dish. "I know ice cream is not generally thought of as nourishing," she said, hoping a little small talk would relax the tension between them, "but actually it is."

"It's bad for the teeth," muttered Clay, ever the consummate dentist. "Too much sugar."

The corners of her mouth twitched upward in a tiny smile. "Yes, I know, sweetheart, but I'll gladly sacrifice a tooth if it will help me make you understand what I'm going to tell you."

"I don't think I'm being difficult or unreasonable," he grated. "Francie is my child now, and I have a right to know her background. The information wasn't available when we adopted her, but now I want to find out these details. Who's her father? Are you still involved with him? Why did you give her up?"

It's true, he wasn't being unreasonable, but he was making it awfully difficult for Tamara. She took a deep breath and hoped her voice would be firm. "I was raped when I was sixteen, and I was barely seventeen when my baby was born."

Clay had picked up his tea. "Raped!" He slammed the glass back down on the table. Tamara's head jerked up in time to see him come out of his chair like a raging bull. "Who raped you? Where is he now?"

There was murder in his eyes, not necessarily directed at her, but it was too much like her father's reaction when she'd told him, and that *had* been directed at her. She cringed and curled up in the corner of the sofa.

"Tamara." Clay lowered his voice as he sat down beside her and cupped her shoulders in his hands. "What's the matter? My God," he rasped, "you didn't think I was going to hit you...?"

Slowly she raised her head to look at him. The blood had drained from his face and he looked stunned. "I...I thought you might," she whispered.

"Did that son of a bitch beat you as well as rape you?" Now his tone was low and filled with fury.

"N-no, not...Grady," she stammered. "He was a lot bigger than I, and insistent, but he didn't hit me or anything. He just wouldn't take no for an answer."

His hands tightened on her arms. "Then who did strike you?"

"My...my father." She began to sob and hid her face in her hands. "He said nice girls don't get raped, and the girls who do ask for it. My mother agreed with him. He...he said he wasn't going to accept a bastard grandchild, and...and if I insisted on keeping the baby I couldn't come back home."

Clay muttered an oath, then lifted her onto his lap. She snuggled in his arms and sobbed softly. He held her and let her cry, murmuring words of comfort now and then, but when she was calm again, he gently but firmly put her down and went back to his own chair. "I'm sorry I scared you, but I wasn't expecting to hear that my wife had been raped. Who was this man? Did the police catch him? If so, is he still in prison?"

She shook her head vigorously. "No, Clay, it wasn't like that. Grady was a teenager, too. He was the son of the mayor of our small town, spoiled and boisterous but not vicious—"

"You don't call rape vicious?" Clay interrupted angrily. "Are you making excuses for him?"

Tamara put her bowl down on the coffee table. "No, of course I'm not." Her tone was heating up, too. "There's no excuse for what he did to me, but don't forget, he's Franie's biological father. He was a young jock who'd been drinking and made a mistake. He even apologized afterward when he realized I was a virgin." She paused to take a deep breath. "I'm sure it never occurred to my parents to call the police. They were too afraid of a scandal, of tarnishing their precious name. Besides, according to them, I'd led him on or he wouldn't have done it."

Clay sank back in his chair. "I see," he said. "Does he know about Francie? Am I going to have to fight him for her, too?"

"I'm not trying to take her away from you," she said, exasperated, "and Grady doesn't know about her. Nobody back home does except my parents and me. My father and mother made sure of that. They sent me away to Fort Worth before I'd even begun to show.

"I never talked to Grady after that night. He graduated from high school that year while I was gone, and by the time I got back he was away at college. Our paths never crossed again."

"Do you know where he is now?" Clay asked. "What he's doing?"

"My mother mentioned a year or so ago that he and the high school principal's daughter had announced their engagement, and that they were both attending law school," Tamara said. "He seems to have turned out okay. You don't have to worry about Francie inheriting any criminal tendencies—"

"I'm not worried about Francie's genes," he interrupted coldly. "Suppose you just go on with the story."

She completed the account in pretty much the same order as she'd told his mother earlier, but when she got to the part about hiring Paul Wallace, the private investigator, Clay stopped her. "Did you authorize that man to use illegal tactics to get the information you wanted?"

Her eyes widened and she glared at him. "Of course not," she said angrily. "How could you even ask such a thing?"

Clay glared back at her. "I'm asking because that's what he did. He bribed an employee at the home where Francie was born to give him confidential information from their records."

Tamara was both shocked and unconvinced. "I don't believe that! Paul wouldn't do such—"

"You'd better believe it," Clay interrupted sternly, then told her about the phone call from his lawyer the day before.

Tamara listened in amazement. "So that's how you found out I was Francie's mother." Her tone was thick with regret, and her whole body ached to hold him and try to relieve some of the pain she'd so thoughtlessly caused him. But she knew she couldn't stand another rejection, so instead she said the only thing she could say. "Oh, darling, I'm so sorry. What a dreadful shock it must have been for you. No wonder you were so upset...."

"Upset? Well, yes, you could say that," he said bitterly, "but there are better ways to describe my state of mind. How about freaked out? Or unhinged? Pulverized has a nice ring—"

Suddenly Tamara couldn't take any more. She clapped her hands over her ears. "Stop it!" she shouted, and scrambled off the sofa. "Dammit, Clay, I'm trying my best to make you understand how sorry I am. How guilty I feel. I'll do anything, anything at all, to make it up to you, but you've got to be willing at least to listen and make an effort to believe—"

Clay was out of his chair and had her in his arms before she could finish. His body was still fresh from the shower, and he smelled of soap as he held her close and rubbed his cheek in her hair. "You're right, my little love," he murmured brokenly, "I'm behaving like a jerk. I'm sorry. Oh, God, I'm so sorry...."

A sob shook him and took her so by surprise that she raised her head to look at him. There were tears in his eyes. A wave of love washed over her, and she put her arms around his waist and hugged him. They were going to have to get this over with, and soon, before they both wound up as emotional basket cases.

For a moment they just stood there wrapped in the embrace—trying to draw strength from each other. Then Clay straightened, and when he spoke his voice was steady once more. "Do you want to continue with your story if I promise to keep my mouth shut and not harass you, or would you rather put it off for some other time? It's up to you."

All Tamara wanted was to get the telling over with, and she said so. They returned to their seats and she went on with her story. It was a long and emotionally draining ordeal, and although Clay had promised not to, he occasionally interrupted to ask a question. However, he accepted her answers without comment. When it was finally over she was exhausted, and she could see that he was, too. For several minutes they sat quietly in the silent room, lost in their own thoughts.

Then Clay looked at his watch and stood up. "I need time to think, Tamara. I'm going back to the ranch to spend the night. Will you be all right here alone? If you'd prefer, I'll register you at a hotel.''

Tamara was greatly disappointed, but she chided herself for expecting him to make an instant decision. Actually it was probably a good sign that he hadn't. If he needed to think it over, it could mean that he wanted to believe her. "I'd rather stay here," she assured him. "I'm not a child. I've had a lot of experience at taking care of myself.''

Tamara slept little that night. She tossed and turned, her overactive imagination keeping her in a state of constant turmoil. Would Clay accept the unvarnished truth as she'd told it and forgive her? Or would he reject it as more lies and...and what? The alternative didn't bear thinking about.

She finally fell asleep a little before daybreak and it was almost nine o'clock before she awoke. She had just finished getting dressed and was halfway down the stairs when she heard Clay's key in the lock. Tense and apprehensive, she waited as the door opened and he stepped into the entryway. The sight of him wasn't reassuring. He looked as bad as she did, tired, with dark circles under his eyes and lines of strain at the corners of his mouth.

Francie wasn't with him.

As if drawn by a magnet, he raised his head and looked up at her on the staircase. "Good morning," he said formally. "Did you sleep well?''

She wasn't going to be coy. "No, I didn't." She continued down the stairs until she stood in front of him.

"Neither did I," he said, and turned toward the living room. "Do you mind if we talk now? I want to get this over with.''

A heavy feeling of dread slowed her steps as she followed him into the big formal room. He motioned her to a chair in front of the window, then took the matching one on the other side of the table between them.

Tamara's gaze met his, and she knew what he was going to say. For some reason it was important that she say it first. "You think I'm still lying to you, don't you?"

He looked away. "I don't know what to believe." His tone was rough with frustration. "I think you're telling the truth about what happened up to the time you gave the baby up for adoption, but I can't accept the idea that you didn't deliberately insinuate yourself into my life in order to make it easier to take Francie away from me at some later date. Also, I can't accept the excuse that you fell in love with me, and being with Francie was just an added bonus—"

"I never said that," Tamara objected. "Being able to help raise my daughter is extremely important to me, but I'd never have said I loved you if I didn't. Besides, you only married me so you could have a housekeeper and a convenient sex partner, so why does it matter to you whether or not I love you?"

He had the grace to wince. "You know it wasn't as cut-and-dried as that, and at least I was honest with you. I didn't claim to love you in order to get what I wanted." He took a deep breath and again captured her gaze. "I'm sorry, Tamara," he said, and there was anguish in his tone, "but our marriage was based on a lie. I'm going to file for an annulment, and I'm asking you to pack up and leave my house as soon as possible."

Chapter Eleven

Tamara was stricken. Literally. She could neither move nor speak, but just sat there numb and mute with grief. This must be the way Clay had felt when he was told that Alicia was dead.

Except that Tamara's loss was twofold. Both her husband and her small daughter. He was sending her away, and she knew that once she'd left, she'd never see either of them again. Clay wouldn't allow it.

There was a whirring sound in her head, and although she could see that he was talking, she couldn't decipher what he was saying. Finally he reached over and put his hand on her arm. The contact snapped her out of her daze. She wished it hadn't, because the ability to function also brought searing pain.

"Tamara, don't look like that," he begged, and there was an edge of fear in his plea. "I wish I could be more forgiving. I've tried but I can't get past the fact that you aren't to be trusted. You lied to me, and deceived me, about everything that was important in our relationship."

When she still didn't speak, he stood and began to pace. "To some extent I can even understand why you did it. I know you love Francie. Since you've been living with me, I've observed you with her, and I'm willing to concede that point, but that makes you all the more dangerous."

He stopped in front of her as if to add emphasis to what he was saying. "You seem to have no conscience when it comes to lying in order to get what you want. If we continued this sham of a marriage, I'd never know when you might tire of pretending you're in love with me and just take Francie and disappear. I won't give you that opportunity."

Tamara sat with her head bowed. She couldn't look up and let him see the agony his words were inflicting. She couldn't even blame him. If their roles were switched and she'd lied and deceived her, she wouldn't trust him again, either.

After a few moments of silence, he hunkered down and placed his hands on her shoulders. "Tamara, are you all right?" he asked urgently. "Are you listening to me? Do you understand what I'm telling you?"

She nodded and cleared her throat. "Yes, I understand." Her voice sounded rusty, as though it hadn't been used lately. "I have no one to blame but myself. I'm just sorry you won't believe that I love you every bit as deeply as I love Francie."

He sighed and put his fingers under her chin to lift her head. "I'm sorry about that, too," he murmured unsteadily as he moved his hand to stroke a lock of hair away from her cheek. "Sorrier than you can possibly imagine." He got to his feet and started to pace again. "I hope for both our sakes that you'll agree to leave within the next few hours. I've canceled all my appointments at the office for today, and Francie is missing school. I think it's important for all three of us, but especially for her, that we get back to normal as soon as possible."

Tamara's head was swimming. This was all happening to
fast. How could she make rational decisions when sh
couldn't think straight? Wasn't he even going to let her se
Francie again? Say goodbye to her? And how would all th
affect the child? Would she think that Tamara had ju
abandoned her? No. She couldn't allow that.

Her mind started functioning again. "Clay, aren't yo
overlooking the problems my sudden departure could caus
for Francie? That's the way she lost her mother, sudden
and with no warning. She seems to have survived that prett
well, but now she thinks of me as a ..." She hesitated. Sh
couldn't say "mother." Clay would never accept tha
"A ... mother figure. If I just disappear out of her life, to
it could do irreparable harm to her self-image."

Clay stopped pacing and stood still for a momen
"Damn, I never thought of that," he admitted. "I agr
that it will make losing you more painful for her, but wh
should it damage her self-esteem?"

Tamara knew she had to be very careful how she handle
this. "Because even at her tender age, Francie will see it a
abandonment. As she gets older and more knowledgeab
about adoption, she'll figure out that she was also aban
doned by the woman who gave her birth. It doesn't take
psychologist to understand the natural progression fro
that. By the time she's in her teens, and probably befor
Francie may well see herself as an unlovable and unwante
child."

Slowly Clay turned to face her. "I admit it sounds rea
sonable, but why should I take your word for it?"

She shook her head sadly. "I don't expect you to, but f
Francie's sake, please talk to a therapist before you send m
away. You must know someone, a patient, friend or neigh
bor who's qualified. Just call and ask about it as a hyp
thetical question. They can at least tell you on the pho
what the potential is for serious damage."

He continued to watch her for a few seconds, then turned
nd walked out of the room.

While Clay was gone, Tamara quickly formulated a plan
) appeal for a few weeks' reprieve. That's all she could hope
or. There was no possibility that he'd change his mind
bout seeking an annulment, but with a lot of prayer and
ick she might be able to make the breakup of their family
ss painful for her vulnerable little daughter. A last gift of
we from the mother Francie didn't even know she had.

When Clay came back into the room, he looked both
erplexed and frustrated. "The child psychologist I called
grees with you. He advises that we give Francie time to
djust to the idea that you may be leaving soon for a lengthy
bsence. Then, after you're gone, the absence can be ex-
nded until I feel she's ready to accept the fact that you're
ot coming back." He slumped down into a chair and
ıbbed his hands over his face. "Dammit all, Tamara. Why
idn't you honor your agreement to stay out of your child's
fe and let the adoptive parents who wanted her raise her?
Vhy didn't you leave Francie and me alone?"

Tamara was asking herself the same thing. "Obviously
'hen I decided to search for my baby, I was thinking with
ıy emotions rather than my good sense. I can only tell you
ıat at the time I set all this in motion it seemed harmless."
he raked her fingers through her hair. "Are you going to
ıke this advice, or do you prefer that I leave now? I'll go
long with whatever you want."

Clay sighed. "What I want isn't the issue here. It's what's
est for Francie. To tell you the truth, I don't know how
ıuch more of this I can take, but the therapist I consulted
; a hell of a lot more knowledgeable than I, so I'd better
ıllow his advice. If you want to stay on for a week or so,
'm willing to play out this little charade, but I'll be damned
I know what candy-coated excuse we can give Francie for
our leaving."

Tamara wasn't sure how much more of this anguish she could stand, either, but she'd grab any opportunity to spend more time with the two people she loved most in all the world. "I'll stay," she said, "and if you'll let me, I'll help you make up a plausible story for us to tell Francie." A bitter chuckle rose in her throat. "After all, you said it yourself. I'm a world-class liar."

Clay left to pick up his daughter at the ranch, and while he was gone, Tamara devised what she hoped was an acceptable reason for returning to Iowa. That evening after Francie was in bed, she talked it over with Clay. He made some suggestions and together they refined it to a believable tale.

When it came time for them to go to bed, things became awkward again. They climbed the stairs together, then paused at the door to their bedroom. Tamara's heart pounded. Would Clay sleep with her?

After a moment's hesitation, she walked into the room and Clay followed. Her body tingled with hope. Maybe he did intend to spend the nights with her. If so, they'd make love. Maybe not tonight, but very soon. They couldn't lie in the same bed and resist the overwhelming swell of desire that bonded them together.

Then Clay spoke. "I'll take the clothes I'll need in the morning and sleep in one of the other bedrooms, then tomorrow I'll move all my things out of here." His tone was brusque.

"No!" The protest was out before she could bite it back and Clay's eyes widened. "That is—" she swallowed and tried again "—I mean, I'm the one who's leaving. There's no need for you to be displaced. I'll move back into the room down the hall."

He looked as if he was going to argue, but then shrugged. "If that's the way you want it," he said and turned away.

It wasn't the way she wanted it. She wanted to share this room, and this bed, with him, but he wasn't about to allow it. He wouldn't even try to work out their problems and find a way to salvage their marriage. Quickly she gathered up her nightclothes and hurried out of the room.

It was a long and dreadful night. Her mind seethed with projections of a dreary future, alone and lonely, with no one to love and no one to love her. She was also tormented by the temptation to go to Clay, to crawl into bed with him and seduce him into making love with her. She knew he couldn't resist for long; the sexual magnetism between them was too strong, even when he'd lost all respect for her. But it wouldn't solve anything, and afterward he'd send her away immediately before it could happen again.

The following morning it was obvious that neither of them had slept much.

That evening after dinner, Tamara told the lie she'd concocted for Francie's benefit, but this time Clay was a co-conspirator. They took the little girl into the library, and Tamara put her arms around her as they sat on the sofa. "Honey, I have something to tell you," she began. "My mother called from Iowa today. She said my dad has had a heart attack and is in the hospital. I might have to go back there if he doesn't get better soon."

Francie looked up at her. "Can me and Daddy go, too?"

Tamara shook her head. "I'm afraid not. Daddy has to work, and you have to go to school."

"But who'll take care of us?" she asked anxiously.

Clay answered that question. "Oh, we'll be well taken care of. Hertha Gross is coming back from New Mexico to be our housekeeper again."

It had been Clay's idea to bring Hertha back, and it was a good one. She'd been the child's nanny from the time Francie was adopted until she retired and Tamara took over. Her return would go a long way to help ease the loss Francie would feel when Tamara left, and Hertha had been happy to oblige when Clay called her.

Apparently full-time retirement hadn't appealed to her after all, but it would be two weeks before she'd be free to leave her daughter's home. Therefore, Tamara couldn't leave San Antonio any earlier than that.

Francie was so delighted to hear Hertha was coming back that the possibility Tamara might have to leave was soon forgotten. However, the seed had been sown and would be nourished by reported phone calls from Iowa at intervals so the youngster would have time to get used to her absence.

The following week was one of conflicting emotions for Tamara. She treasured the time spent with her daughter. It was precious beyond measure, and when they were together she refused to look beyond those moments.

It was also depressing and upsetting. Clay kept her at a distance, not just physically but emotionally, as well. He spoke to her only when necessary, and what little time they had together was spent in silence or in conversation with Francie. At night they went to bed in their separate rooms, and more often than not, Tamara cried herself to sleep.

Although Clay and Tamara never spoke harshly or raised their voices, the atmosphere in the home was chilly and devoid of laughter. Tamara hoped Francie was too young to pick up on it, but was afraid she did.

Once she asked her father with obvious concern if he was "mad at Tamara." Both he and Tamara denied it vigorously, and after that Clay was more cordial when the child was there. However, it apparently didn't convince her because later she asked Tamara, in Clay's presence, why she didn't sleep with her daddy anymore. That rattled them both to the extent that they stammered and stuttered trying to come up with an answer that would satisfy a bright eight-year-old without upsetting her.

"I don't sleep well with someone else in the bed," Clay said.

"But you and Mommy always slept together," Francie reminded him.

Tamara knew her face was flaming. "I...I'm not used to sharing a bed, and I'm more comfortable in a room by myself," she said, getting Clay off the hook. It was a lie, but then lies were coming more easily to her now.

Together they'd managed to soothe that anxiety, but only temporarily. In the very early morning hours of Tuesday, ten days after the initial explosion that destroyed their marriage, Tamara was startled awake by a loud, high-pitched scream, which chilled her to the core. "Mommy! Mommy! No! No! Please, Mommy!"

It was Francie screaming with terror.

Tamara jumped out of bed and tore through the adjoining bathroom into Francie's bedroom just as Clay raced through the hall door. He reached the bed first and picked the writhing child up in his arms although she pummeled him with her fists.

"Mommy, Mommy," she moaned as Clay gently but firmly shook her awake. "I want my mommy."

"Francie, sweetheart, wake up," Clay said gently as he sat down on the side of the bed with her in his lap. "Daddy's here. It's all right. It's only a bad dream."

In spite of her shock and fear, Tamara recognized that this situation was not new to Clay. He was handling it quite knowledgeably, as if it had happened many times before. Francie woke up gradually and clung to Clay as she sobbed and shivered with terror. He held her and comforted her.

Tamara faded into the background and watched as Clay lovingly calmed his overwrought daughter. She was overwhelmingly moved by the tenderness with which he handled this traumatic episode, and her love for him swelled until it was almost more than she could contain. She'd never have to worry about her little girl. She knew beyond doubt that Clay would do whatever was necessary to keep Francie safe and happy.

Quietly she returned to her own room, put on her robe and slippers and went downstairs. Although there was a definite chill in the night air at this time of the year in Iowa, here in San Antonio the weather was still balmy. She opened the front door, then deactivated the night lock and stepped out onto the porch. There was no need for a light. The full moon and twinkling stars provided a soft glow of illumination. Sitting down in one of the big wicker basket chairs, she drew her feet up to the seat and wrapped her arms around her legs, then rested her chin on her knees.

Tamara had some serious thinking to do, and it had to be done now. Her legitimate effort to gain more time with Clay and Francie before leaving San Antonio for good wasn't working out the way it was supposed to.... ;

She was so lost in thought that she didn't hear Clay coming downstairs until the sound of his voice calling her name snapped her back to awareness. "I'm out here on the porch, Clay," she called, and in seconds the outside light flashed on and he opened the screen.

"Dammit, Tamara, I've been looking all over for you," he scolded. "Why didn't you tell me you were coming out here?"

She raised her head and looked at him with surprise. "It didn't occur to me that you'd want to know," she said.

He sighed and switched the light off again, then walked over and sat down in the twin chair to hers nearby. "Don't play games with me," he said wearily, and rubbed his eyes.

She put her feet on the floor and sat up straight. "I'm not playing games," she assured him. "Is Francie all right now? Did you get her back to sleep?"

He nodded. "Yes, to both questions. She should be okay now."

"Tonight isn't the first time this happened, is it?" It wasn't really a question.

"No, it's not," he confirmed. "After Alicia's sudden death, Francie started having nightmares. She dreams that her mother is gone and she's terrified when she can't find her. I took her to a therapist, the same one I talked to last week. It took several months, but by the time you came to us she was no longer having either the dreams or the therapy."

A wave of guilt nearly overwhelmed Tamara. "And now it's started up again," she murmured. "Why didn't you tell me she'd had nightmares after her mother's death when I suggested we postpone my leaving here?"

He shrugged. "It didn't seem germane."

"But it might have been—"

Clay interrupted. "Tamara, remember I talked to her therapist at that time as you suggested. We didn't discuss the nightmares, but he felt strongly that you shouldn't just disappear from her life the way she perceived Alicia as having done. None of us could have foreseen this complication."

Tamara wasn't reassured. She now felt strongly that she should have left when Clay had told her to and let him deal with any problem it might have caused for Francie, but she hadn't. Now it was time for her to get out of their lives before she caused any more damage.

She took a deep breath and hoped she could keep her voice steady. "Maybe not," she said uncertainly, "but since my plan is obviously causing the poor child to have nightmares again, I can see only one solution. After Francie leaves for school in the morning, I'll pack my things and go back to Iowa."

Clay blinked, then stared at her in the moonlight. "You'll what?" He sounded as shocked as if he'd never asked her to leave.

"I know it will be inconvenient for you if I don't wait until Hertha gets here," she said, "but I won't subject my daughter to any more trauma than she's already experienced. She's expecting me to have to leave suddenly, so it won't come as a total shock to her, and before long she'll forget all about me."

"Sure she will," he said grimly. "She'll forget all about you the same way I will."

She winced. He was being sarcastic, but he was really only speaking the truth. Once she had gone and Hertha came back, they'd forget about her quickly enough. *But how was she going to survive for the rest of her life without them?*

"Exactly," she agreed. "In the meantime, surely you have friends or neighbors she can stay with after school until you get home from the office."

He didn't answer, but got up and walked to the porch railing, where he stood looking out toward the lighted street with his back to her. "Why are you so all fired eager to leave now?" he asked gruffly. "When we first talked about it, you were sure it would be a mistake to subject Francie to another 'abandonment' as you put it."

"I was wrong," Tamara said sorrowfully, "but that's nothing new. I can't seem to do anything right where she's concerned."

"Why do you think you were wrong?"

"Because her nightmares came back. I hadn't foreseen that she'd pick up on the tension between you and me. That was a grave error. She not only recognized it, but it frightened her."

"And you're the only one in this household qualified to make errors?"

"Apparently so," she said heatedly, stung by his taunting. "At least I'm the only one who does. You and Francie were doing just fine until I came along."

He grunted. "We were surviving, but that's about all." He turned around and looked down at her. "What makes you so positive that if you rush away now that her nightmares have come back, it won't traumatize her even more?"

His supposition was like a knife in her heart. "Dammit, Clay," she cried as she jumped to her feet, "are you deliberately baiting me? I'm not sure of anything, and I'm through playing amateur psychologist with my child's well-being." This time she turned away from him as she lowered her voice and continued. "I've found the answers I came here looking for. The baby I gave away eight years ago is much better off with you than she would ever have been with me. You're a fabulous father. She's healthy, happy and secure. You did an excellent job of guiding her through the turmoil of her mother's death until I stumbled into your lives and bungled them up again—" Her voice broke, and she clutched the railing as she took a deep breath. "Why are you arguing about my decision to leave early, Clay? Ten days ago you couldn't get rid of me fast enough. You don't want me here. You hate me—"

Again her voice broke, and for a few seconds they were surrounded by silence. Then Clay spoke, and his tone was low and reluctant. "I don't hate you, Tamara. I love you."

She blinked, then gasped as his words connected with her disbelieving mind. "You...you *love* me?" She turned toward him.

He stood little more than an arm's length away from her, but his expression was both mournful and forbidding. If he meant what he'd just said, he wasn't happy about it.

"I'm afraid so," he admitted sadly. "Why do you think I reacted so violently when I learned that you'd been deceiving me? It was then I first realized that in your sweet and loving way you'd managed not only to integrate yourself into my home and my life, but into my heart and soul, as well." He looked away from her. "It damn near killed me," he murmured in little more than a whisper.

Tamara could only stand there, blinded by tears and mute with grief. She'd finally earned Clay's love only to have it snatched away from her by her own well-meaning but nevertheless devious scheming.

"How's that for irony?" he mused. "I was so sure I'd never love any other woman as deeply as I loved Alicia that I couldn't face up to my feelings for you until it was too late."

Tamara felt dizzy and disoriented. "Too...too late?"

He nodded. "I'm afraid so. A successful marriage has to be based on trust, and I can no longer trust you. I wish I could. I've tried, but..."

Tamara knew that she'd lost more than just Clay's love. Along with it she'd lost any chance at happiness. She'd never again have the husband, home and family she'd so recently started with Clay and Francie. That was all she needed to keep her happy, but only Clay was able to provide it, and he wouldn't. Couldn't.

She reached up and pushed back a strand of hair that had fallen over her forehead. "I'm going back to bed," she said as she walked slowly toward the door. "I'll need more sleep if I'm going to start a long trip in a few hours. I'll get Francie off to school, but you'll have to arrange to be here when she comes home. Tell her whatever you think is best to explain my absence."

Tamara tossed and turned but slept little for the rest of the night. She heard Clay's footsteps out in the hall once, and lay breathlessly still, hoping and praying that he'd open her door and come in. He didn't, and she chastised herself for being such a hopeless romantic. She dozed off toward morning, and when the alarm awakened her and she went downstairs, both Clay and his car were gone.

She treasured her last moments with Francie while she fixed breakfast and helped her get ready for school. After Tamara had gone, she wanted the child to remember this time as a happy one, so she kept the mood lighthearted as they talked, told each other jokes and sang silly songs.

All went well until just a few minutes before the school bus was due, then Tamara felt the rise of panic. It wouldn't do to break down now. Francie didn't know yet that Tamara was leaving, and Tamara didn't want her to know until she came home that afternoon.

She knelt down to help Francie put on her sweater, then forced a bright smile. "How about a big, sloppy, extra-special hug and kiss before you leave?" she said.

Francie giggled. "You mean bigger, sloppier and extra specialer than usual?" she asked.

Tamara nodded, knowing she couldn't trust the lump in her throat to let her speak.

"Okay," Francie said with a wide grin and threw her arms around Tamara. It was a bone-crushing embrace, and Francie's warm, soft little lips burned Tamara's cheek.

"Always remember that I love you very, very much," she said as she embraced her daughter for the last time. "Don't ever forget that, will you?"

The swoosh of air brakes alerted them to the bus stopping at the curb outside, and Francie pulled away. "I love you, too," she called happily as she rushed out the door to the waiting vehicle.

Tamara walked out to the porch and watched until the bus was out of sight. She felt dried up and old. A wild crying jag would have been welcomed as a necessary release, but she had no more sobs, and all of her tears had been spilled. Now there was nothing left to do but pack her things and leave father and daughter to pick up the pieces of the mess she'd made of their lives.

Several hours later, Tamara was upstairs haphazardly packing her clothes into suitcases, more interested in speed than in neatness. Now that she'd made up her mind to go, she wanted to do it quickly before she had time to dwell on the life she was leaving behind.

Since she'd always lived in Iowa, she'd assumed she'd return there, but on second thought, there was no real reason for her to do that. Except for her parents, from whom she was estranged, there was nothing for her to go back to. She'd resigned her job and given up her apartment when she'd married Clay.

She had no responsibilities. No one cared where or how she lived. With winter coming on, maybe she'd stay in the warm Southern states. Florida, or Arizona. She was a teacher, and a good one. She could work anywhere and she had a nice nest egg to live on until she could find a position.

She was so immersed in her chaotic thoughts and her compulsive need to hurry that she didn't hear the car drive up to the house, or the front door open and shut, so she was startled when Clay's voice called to her from downstairs. "Tamara! Tamara, are you here? Answer me!" He sounded almost frantic.

She shook with relief as she went to the hall and called down, "I'm upstairs, Clay."

Thank God he wasn't going to let her leave without saying goodbye. Even though it would be awkward and difficult for him— and agony for her—she needed the closure, that tangible end of their relationship in order to deal with it.

He took the steps two at a time and looked somewhat wild-eyed and harried as he came down the hall toward her. "I... I was afraid you'd already left," he said as if that explained his strange behavior.

"No, I'm still packing, but I won't be much longer," she assured him and went back into the bedroom.

He followed and looked around as she resumed her task. "I was called to the hospital at six o'clock this morning. An emergency with one of my patients," he explained. "I was only just now able to leave."

That would have been when she heard him in the hall. She'd probably been awakened by the telephone but hadn't been aware of it. She was glad her back was to him. She didn't want him to see how much it meant to her that he hadn't wanted to let her go away without seeing her off.

"I'm sorry you were called out so early," she said softly. "You couldn't have gotten more than three or four hours' sleep what with being wakened by Francie, too."

For a moment he didn't respond. When he did, she thought she heard a tremor in his voice. "After the way I've treated you, I wouldn't expect you to care if I ever slept again."

She dropped the bra she was folding and turned around. He was leaning against the wall and looked tired and...and what? *Defeated* was the word that came to mind. "Of course I care," she assured him, and there was definitely a quaver in her tone. "Why don't you go back to bed? Your receptionist has probably already canceled all your morning appointments—"

"Tamara, don't leave me." He spoke so softly she could hardly hear him.

She blinked. "I...I beg your pardon?"

He raised his head and looked directly into her eyes. "Please don't leave me, sweetheart." His voice was raw with anguish. "I know I've been acting like a jackass, but I'll do everything I can to make up for it."

She still couldn't grasp what he was getting at. "I don't understand. You told me to leave. You don't want me—"

"I want you so much that I don't think I can survive if I lose you," he said flatly. "I can't excuse the way I've been behaving. I guess I went a little crazy when I learned that you were Francie's birth mother. I was afraid you'd only married me so you could be with her. That you didn't love me at all but were just using me—"

"But you must know that's not true!" Tamara said, still confused. "I've told you and shown you in every way I could that I love you."

"I know, but I was determined not to believe it," he admitted regretfully. "I'd been so sure I could never love again after Alicia that I wouldn't admit my burgeoning feelings for you. It somehow seemed disloyal to her. I kept pushing them away, denying them, even after you and I were married, when anyone but an idiot could see that I adored you. That I desperately needed the love and care you so generously lavished on me."

Tamara stood staring at him, speechless and confused. She couldn't believe he was saying all the things she'd longed to hear but never expected to.

Slowly he raised his arms and started toward her.

Without hesitation, she walked into his embrace, and his arms closed around her, cuddling her against him. "Mmm," he murmured, "I've been so hungry to hold you like this that it became an unrelenting physical ache, but even then I resisted. I didn't want to fall in love with you. The pain of losing Alicia overwhelmed me. I didn't want to risk that happening again."

She felt the tremors that shook him and realized that she was trembling, too, as they stood clinging to each other.

"Up until last night, I'd been the one to decide whether you stayed or whether you left," he continued. "Oh, I told myself I was going to banish you for good, but then I kept finding excuses to postpone it. Francie would be upset. Then Hertha couldn't come until later.

"But the balance of power suddenly changed after Francie's nightmare. You announced that you were leaving. Not sometime in the indefinite future but within a few hours, and you would no longer listen to my excuses for postponing it."

He gently rubbed one hand over her back, then brought it to rest at the firm rise of her derriere. "It wasn't until then that I finally woke up to the fact that I didn't have any say whether I fell in love or not. I was already deeply, passionately and irrevocably in love with you. If I lost you, I'd not only roast in hell, but it would also be my own damn fault for being such a stubborn mule."

His hand moved farther down and pushed her into the hardness of his need for her. She stood on her toes and twined her arms around his neck as she moved sensuously against him, eliciting a groan from deep in his throat.

"Are you saying you want me to stay?" she murmured.

"Sweetheart, I'm begging you to stay." His voice was unsteady. "I want you so much that I'm not above offering a bribe. We'll tell Francie you're her real mother."

Tamara knew what a huge concession that offer was for Clay to make, and she loved him all the more for his willingness to do it for her.

She nuzzled the hollow at the base of his throat. "I can't tell you how much I appreciate your thoughtfulness, darling. But it's not necessary. I'm staying because I love you and want to be with you always, not just because I love Francie. We'll find the right way and time to tell her about me. Now, though, do you have any objection to getting started on those brothers and sisters we promised her?"

He moved his hand up to stroke the side of her breast and sent prickles down her spine. "Do you mean *right now?*" he asked, and there was a wicked gleam in his eyes, "or now, meaning at this time in our marriage?"

"Right now!" she said huskily and pivoted against him again.

He shivered and swept her up in his arms. "Your bed or mine?"

"Ours," she whispered and nibbled at his earlobe as he carried her toward the master bedroom.

*   *   *   *   *

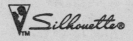

**This March rediscover
a forgotten love with**

by Request™

missing memories

Is the power of love strong enough to bring back a past that has been forgotten?

Three complete novels by your favorite authors—in one special collection!

TALL IN THE SADDLE by Mary Lynn Baxter
FORGOTTEN DREAM by Paula Detmer Riggs
HAWK'S FLIGHT by Annette Broadrick

The path to love can be treacherous...especially if you don't remember the way!

**Available wherever
Harlequin and Silhouette books are sold.**

HARLEQUIN®   *Silhouette*®

SAME TIME, NEXT YEAR
Debbie Macomber
(SE #937, February)

Midnight, New Year's Eve...a magical night with
Summer Lawton that James Wilken knew could never
be enough. So he'd spontaneously asked her to meet
him again in exactly one year's time. Now that time
had come...and with it, a friendly reunion that was
quickly turning to love!

Don't miss
SAME TIME, NEXT YEAR,
by Debbie Macomber,
available in February!

She's friend, wife, mother—she's you! And beside
each Special Woman stands a wonderfully
special man. It's a celebration of our heroines—
and the men who become part of their lives.

Don't miss **THAT SPECIAL WOMAN!** each month—
from some of your special authors! Only from
Silhouette Special Edition!

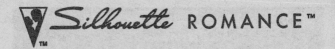

Silhouette ROMANCE™

BELIEVING IN MIRACLES
by
Linda Varner

Carpenter Andy Fulbright and Honorine "Honey" Truman had all the criteria for a perfect marriage—they liked and respected each other, they desired and needed each other...and *neither* one loved the other! But with the help of some mistletoe and two young elves, these two might learn to believe in the miracle of Christmas....

BELIEVING IN MIRACLES is the second book in Linda Varner's MR. RIGHT, INC., a heartwarming series about three hardworking bachelors in the building trade who find love at first sight—construction site, that is!

Don't miss BELIEVING IN MIRACLES, available in December. And look for Book 3, WIFE MOST UNLIKELY, in March 1995. Read along as old friends make the difficult transition to lovers....

Only from Silhouette®

where passion lives.

SILHOUETTE... Where Passion Lives

Don't miss these Silhouette favorites by some of our most distinguished authors! And now you can receive a discount by ordering two or more titles!

SD#05786	QUICKSAND by Jennifer Greene	$2.89	☐
SD#05795	DEREK by Leslie Guccione	$2.99	☐
SD#05818	NOT JUST ANOTHER PERFECT WIFE by Robin Elliott	$2.99	☐
IM#07505	HELL ON WHEELS by Naomi Horton	$3.50	☐
IM#07514	FIRE ON THE MOUNTAIN by Marion Smith Collins	$3.50	☐
IM#07559	KEEPER by Patricia Gardner Evans	$3.50	☐
SSE#09879	LOVING AND GIVING by Gina Ferris	$3.50	☐
SSE#09892	BABY IN THE MIDDLE by Marie Ferrarella	$3.50 U.S. $3.99 CAN.	☐ ☐
SSE#09902	SEDUCED BY INNOCENCE by Lucy Gordon	$3.50 U.S. $3.99 CAN.	☐ ☐
SR#08952	INSTANT FATHER by Lucy Gordon	$2.75	☐
SR#08984	AUNT CONNIE'S WEDDING by Marie Ferrarella	$2.75	☐
SR#08990	JILTED by Joleen Daniels	$2.75	☐

(limited quantities available on certain titles)

AMOUNT	$_____
DEDUCT: 10% DISCOUNT FOR 2+ BOOKS	$_____
POSTAGE & HANDLING ($1.00 for one book, 50¢ for each additional)	$_____
APPLICABLE TAXES*	$_____
TOTAL PAYABLE (check or money order—please do not send cash)	$_____

To order, complete this form and send it, along with a check or money order for the total above, payable to Silhouette Books, to: **In the U.S.**: 3010 Walden Avenue, P.O. Box 9077, Buffalo, NY 14269-9077; **In Canada**: P.O. Box 636, Fort Erie, Ontario, L2A 5X3.

Name:_____

Address:_____ City:_____

State/Prov.:_____ Zip/Postal Code:_____

*New York residents remit applicable sales taxes.
Canadian residents remit applicable GST and provincial taxes.

SBACK-DF

▼ Silhouette®
TM